TAGGED

Diane C. Mullen

ini Charlesbridge

Published by Charlesbridge
85 Main Street
Watertown, MA 02472
(617) 926-0329
www.charlesbridge.com

Library of Congress Cataloging-in-Publication Data
Mullen, Diane C., author.
  Tagged / Diane C. Mullen.
    pages cm
    Summary: When Liam, a fourteen-year-old graffiti artist, can't keep his
grades up and is threatened by a local gang in the projects of Minneapolis,
his mother sends him to Lake Michigan for the summer.
    ISBN 978-1-58089-583-5 (reinforced for library use)
    ISBN 978-1-60734-569-5 (ebook)
    ISBN 978-1-60734-714-9 (ebook pdf)
1. Graffiti artists—Juvenile fiction. 2. Brothers—Juvenile fiction.
3. Juvenile delinquency—Juvenile fiction. 4. Gangs—Minnesota—
Minneapolis—Juvenile fiction. 5. Families—Minnesota—Minneapolis—
Juvenile fiction. 6. Minneapolis (Minn.)—Juvenile fiction. [1. Graffiti—
Fiction 2. Brothers—Fiction. 3. Juvenile delinquency—Fiction. 4. Gangs—
Fiction. 5. Family life—Minnesota—Minneapolis—Fiction. 6. Minneapolis
(Minn.)—Fiction.] I. Title.

PZ7.M912Tag 2015
813.6—dc23   2013049032

Printed in the United States of America
(hc) 10 9 8 7 6 5 4 3 2 1

Display type set in Sonica Brush
Text type set in Candara
Color separations by Colourscan Print Co Pte Ltd, Singapore
Printed by Berryville Graphics in Berryville, Virginia, USA
Production supervision by Brian G. Walker
Designed by Martha MacLeod Sikkema

For Kelly Easton,

beloved mentor who told me I am an Artist

Every act of creation is first an act of destruction.

—Pablo Picasso

—

INTRODUCING MY NEW ME

I'm getting my tag up. All over my Minneapolis hood.

Everyone notices the Saint. St. B.

Empty walls wait to see what I have to say.

I let my Sharpie marker do the talking. On concrete benches at the JFK projects. Sides of metal Dumpsters behind buildings. Bulletproof shelters at bus stops. Cracked brick walls in alleys. On the plexiglass case for crap advertisements at the light-rail station. Everyone knows I'm here.

Got my tagging routine down. Like a graffiti science.

Find the spot.

Look all around.

Silver Sharpie out of my backpack.

Look again.

Now. Press the tip against the wall. Silver ink invades the surface.

ST. B

Done.

Yep. I exist.

FOLLOWING MY OLDER BROTHER

Why? Haven't seen him since he moved out. Tonight he showed up at the park. Said he had a good opportunity for me. Yeah, right.

"What do you want, Kieran?"

"Money, a car, and a nice crib, Liam." He laughs.

Black-and-white screams by. Kieran pulls his Boston Celtics hoodie up. Hides his face from the Minneapolis police.

"Later, po-po." He spits.

We walk. Past the JFKs. John F. Kennedy towers. Kennedy projects. Four concrete buildings with twenty-five floors each. Public housing. My home. I need to get back there. It's almost dark.

"What do you want from me?"

"Just checking in." He shoves me. "How's it going, St. B?"

"What?" No way.

"Yeah, I know it's you, bro." We stop in front of the liquor store. Light flicks off and on. "But I'm not a snitch."

Relieved. "What's the opportunity?" I'm curious.

"You think you're good enough to tag something cooler than just your graffiti name?"

Shrug. St. B is more than just a name.

Cross the street. Some guys are drinking forties hidden in paper bags. They nod at Kieran.

"Want to move up from Sharpie markers to spray paint?" he says.

"Maybe." Love the smell of Sharpies. Dying to use spray paint. "Why?"

"Irish Mafia needs a tag." He throws up his gang's hand sign. "You're the only tagger I actually know."

Too bad I don't want to be just a tagger. "Maybe I'm an artist," I say.

"Sure you are, homie." He laughs. "I've seen your *St. B* around the hood. It's decent. But you're no artist."

Silence.

We round the corner.

Who cares what he thinks? Spray paint's on my mind.

"Where do you want me to do the tag?"

"Cool. We're almost there," he says.

Head to the other side of the block. Stop at the corner market.

He looks around. Points to the sidewall. "Right here." Chews his fingernail.

There's a fresh coat of white paint on the wall. Gang tags bleed through like old melted crayons. A faded red tag for Bloods is covered with shiny silver for Los Crooks—the hated rivals of my brother's Irish Mafia crew.

Wait. "Isn't this Los Crooks stomping ground?"

"It's all good. Besides, I told the guys you'd do it."

"Before you even asked me?"

"Listen, I'm going to get my ass kicked if you don't do this tag. Seriously."

I shrug.

"Here." He shoves a can toward me.

It's Molotow Premium in Juice Green. What the pros use. Very cool color.

"You're good, then?"

I read the directions on the can. Much more involved than a Sharpie. "What do you want me to tag?"

"A shamrock."

Nod.

"Thanks, bro. I won't forget this."

"No big deal." At least I get to spray a tag.

"And make sure it covers all of that new Los Crooks tag."

"What?" My chest tightens. "Really?"

"That's the whole point. Don't be stupid."

"You need to stay here, Kieran." I look all around. "Just in case."

"Yeah, I'm keeping my eyes open." He walks away. "I'll be in the alley."

"But . . ."

"Trust me. I got your back, Liam." He rounds the corner.

I step out of the light.

Shake the can. *CLIKCLAKCLIKCLAKCLIKCLAK.* Mix the paint. Wrench the plastic cap off.

"Kieran?"

"SHUT UP AND DO THE DAMN TAG. I don't have all night."

"Okay." Look again. Now. Press down on the nozzle. *PSSSSSSSSSSSSSSSSSSSSSSSSSSST.*

Hate this smell.

FINISHING THE SHAMROCK

It's harder to do than *St. B.*

Fill in the stem. *PSSSSSSSSSSSSSSSSSSSSSSSSSSST.* Very cool.

Wait. What are those shuffling sounds? Footsteps.

"Kieran?"

Hurry up. Finish. Get out of here.

A guy steps out of the shadows. He's wearing a black-and-silver Oakland Raiders jersey. Chicago White Sox hat. Definitely Los Crooks.

"Irish Mafia's trying to take over Los Crooks territory, huh?" He holds a cell phone out toward me.

"What the . . . ?"

"Smile, shorty." A flash goes off. "You and your bangers are done, man."

"No!" I throw the spray can. Hits him in the head.

He stumbles. "You're DEAD, fool!"

Grab the Juice Green. Run. Around the corner. Into the alley. Pitch-black. *"Kieran?"* He's gone. Crap.

I run. Need to hide somewhere. I head up and over a chain-link fence. Crouch down behind some bushes. Sharp branches shred my shirt, my skin.

Tug on the holy medal around my neck. "Saint Brendan, pray for me."

Los Crooks guy runs into the alley.

I wait. In complete silence. Heart's pounding. Don't even breathe.

"I'll find you, man!" He runs past me. "Count on it!" Turns left. Down the street.

Looking up at the moonless sky, I find the tower lights. The JFKs. I wait . . . then run.

I've got to get home.

SNEAKING INTO THE APARTMENT

Mom's asleep on the couch. TV on. No sound.

Don't wake her up. Carefully walk into the kitchen. Chug a huge cup of water. Calm down. My back stings.

"Liam?"

Great. "Yeah?"

"Did you just get home?"

"I'm getting a drink, Mom."

"Really? It's almost midnight."

"Yep. Want me to turn the TV off?"

"I've got it. Good night, then."

"'Night." What a night.

In our bedroom I can't see anything. Patrick and Declan are snoring. Flick the switch.

"Turn the light off!" Patrick throws his pillow. "I'm trying to sleep."

"Give me a minute." I hang my shirt on the doorknob. It's torn. Bloody.

He sits up. "What time is it?"

"Almost midnight." Wish I'd been asleep two hours ago.

"Hey, what's all that stuff?" Points at me.

"What?"

"All over your hand."

Juice Green paint. "Nothing." How will I make this dis-appear?

"But . . ."

"Don't worry about it." I flick the lights off and hand him his pillow. "Go back to sleep."

SPEAKING WITHOUT A SOUND

I open my blackbook—what the graffiti pros call their sketchbooks. Love this thing. Mom's artist friend sent it. Very cool birthday gift. Practice my graffiti every day. This is my place to take chances. Rehearse. My way to say what I want. Prove I exist.

Surrounded by colors in my hood, I sketch things from the JFKs. People. City buses. Gangs. Food. Light-rail trains. Buildings. Clothes.

Today it's a little girl playing three-on-three at the basketball court. Red LeBron James jersey hangs over her long dress. Yesterday it was Accordion Man. Standing on his usual corner, wearing a dirty brown suit and pink women's slippers.

Always something to draw. Always something about to happen.

Never stop sketching. Want to be able to do more complicated tags. Show that I'm more than just a tagger. Practice the art and become a graffiti writer. Want to create something cool. Something beautiful. Maybe something that's not considered vandalism. And not for Irish Mafia.

Trying to forget about that shamrock.

And Los Crooks.

FIELDING GROUNDERS

I'm on Saint Aloysius Gonzaga High School's varsity team. Today's our first practice at the plush Crusaders Field. Minnesota Twins could play here.

"This one's going to Liam at shortstop," Coach says. "Look alive, infield."

Heart pounding. Tug on my holy medal. For good luck.

"Better be ready." Senior at third base laughs. He looks at my cleats. "Hood rep."

"Worry about yourself." I'm up on my toes. In ready position. "Burb clone."

"What'd you say, O'Malley?"

CRACK! Ball heads toward me. One hop. Scoop it up. Crisp throw to first. Try not to smile.

"Lucky play, freshman." The junior playing second glares at me. "No room for mistakes. You're not playing with your homeboys now."

Homeboys?

"Okay. Let's turn a double play." Coach points with the bat. "Short to second to first."

"Understand that, *ghet-to* boy?" Third baseman keeps running his mouth.

I look toward him. "What the . . . ?"

CRACK!

Ball ricochets off my glove. Bounces over my head. Crap. I never miss line drives.

My teammates laugh.

Left fielder throws the ball in. "Hey, Coach. Get us a shortstop who belongs here."

LIGHTING THE CANDLES

It's my job at dinner every night.

"I wanna help with the matches," Declan says.

"No. You're only five. Have to wait until you're older."

"Patrick's twelve. How come he doesn't get to light the candles?"

"Because I do," I say. But I let Declan blow out the match.

"I won't tell Mom."

"I'll teach you when you're older."

Mom, Patrick, and Fiona sit down at the table with us.

"Okay, grace." Mom bows her head.

I have to lean across to reach Patrick's hand. There's an empty chair between us. It was Dad's. A very long time ago.

"In the name of the Father, and of the Son, and of the Holy Spirit, Amen. Bless us, O Lord, and these thy gifts. . . ." I say the words without thinking.

Look over at that empty chair. After we left Dad, Kieran started sitting in it. Then Kieran left a couple of months ago. Mom changed the locks after he snuck back in. Stole her antique jewelry. Nobody wants to claim that cursed chair. So we lean instead.

"Okay, what did everyone learn at school today?" Mom's usual dinner question.

Usually too much talking.

"Mrs. A. teached us about the tyrannosaurus," Declan says.

Loved sketching dinosaurs when I was five. Dad threw my crayons away. Told me, "Only sissies waste their time drawing."

Declan lifts his hands like claws.

"Does it like hamburgers or hot dogs better?" Mom smiles.

"*Mom*, it doesn't like any of those things. A T. rex eats other animals."

"Hamburgers and hot dogs *are* other animals," Patrick says.

A big bowl of Kraft mac and cheese sits in the middle of the table. Made with water. End of the month. Mom's pay from her two jobs gone. Same with the food stamps.

Fiona raises her hand. "I passed my cursive writing test. Now I can write all my work in cursive. Even math. And I can pass on to fourth grade."

"Good job." Mom gives a thumbs-up. "I don't even know if I remember how to write in cursive anymore. Isn't that sad?"

"Yeah, you're really sad, Mom," Patrick teases.

Maybe I could tag in cursive. Not *St. B.* But maybe something new.

"What about you, lads?" Mom looks at Patrick. Then me.

Shrug. Take a bite of peas. Got dissed at baseball practice.

She stares.

"Um . . ." Patrick starts in. "We just finished *The Giver* in English."

Decent book. Good ending.

"Now we have to work in groups to create fake communities with rules and stuff."

Kieran says rules are a bunch of horseshit. Unless the gang sets them. But he didn't do a tag for Irish Mafia.

"Earth to Liam!" Fiona clangs a fork against her plate.

"Me?"

Declan laughs. Water sprays out of his nose.

"Sick!" Fiona shoves Declan.

Mom sighs. Cleans it up with an old shirt.

"Yuck, I can still see some cheesy snotty stuff on the table." Fiona covers her eyes.

"Knock it off, Fiona." Patrick plugs his ears. "I'm trying to eat, and you keep putting the thought back into my mind."

"Enough." Mom looks at Fiona. "How about you, Liam?"

"I don't know." Know that I hate being at Saint Al's.

"You didn't learn one single thing in school today?"

"Ummm. Studied Pablo Picasso's work in art." Amazing. "Cubism."

"Cubism?" Patrick scoops up the last of his mac and cheese. "What's that?"

"It's when a painting is made of mixed-up pieces. So you have to look at it as a whole in order to understand it." Would love to create something like Picasso.

"Sounds interesting," Mom says.

Very cool. "It was okay."

HANGING OUT WITH MY FRIENDS

Me. Tyrell. Sean. In the courtyard of the JFKs. Showing off for some girls.

Always the same. Throw punches. Pretend to be boxers. Girls laugh. Move around the concrete benches. Girls say, "Oh my God." It's fun for a while. Then someone actually lands a punch. Embarrassing. Girls say, "Ooooh." Someone punches back. Hard. Things get heated.

CLANG! Window slams against a metal frame. We all look to see what tower the noise came from. Praying it's from someone else's apartment. Someone else's mom.

"Tyrell! You told me your homework was done. Get up here right now and finish all this."

"I've got to use the internet, Mom. Got to go to the library first."

"Then why are you standing down there?"

SLAM. We bust out laughing.

"You heard the woman." Tyrell grabs his Joe Mauer jersey. "And when I get upstairs she's going to remind me, again, that I'm not going to get to college hanging around with you knuckleheads. Later."

I remember I'm supposed to read *The Chocolate War* for English.

We move over to the playground. Rusty equipment. Broken swings. Back to punching.

For the girls.

CHATTING WITH THE DEAN

Pulled out of freshman Latin. Great. Now I'll be behind in another class.

"Liam, I wanted to talk with you to see how things are going." She smiles. "Is that okay?"

"I guess." Do I have a choice?

"So, how are things at home?"

"LosCrookssawmedoingatag." Not that she'd care.

"Would you speak slower, please?"

"I said, so good; it's all in the bag." Too much talking.

She stares. "Hmmm." Opens a file. "It looks like you need to put more effort into your academic work."

Check my fingernails.

"I know you're a bright young man. Your standardized test scores are above average, and your grades from Most Holy Trinity were very good."

Nod. That was last year. MHT was a completely different school from Saint Al's.

"So . . . what's going on? You've got a C average right now."

"I've got an A in art." Only class I like. Wish I could major in art.

"That's fine, but your other classes are more important. You're going to be ineligible to play baseball."

"Oh." Who cares?

"I've got updates from your teachers telling me that you have numerous missing assignments. Why aren't you doing your homework?"

"Don't know." Don't have a computer at home. Don't have money to buy supplies for class projects. Don't feel like doing it. Don't belong at this school.

"Well, you're going to have to get your GPA back up to an acceptable level. Until then I have to put you on academic probation. We have strict guidelines here at Saint Al's."

"Right." Like all students must be dropped off by two parents in a Benz?

"Remember, I'm here to help. If you ever want to talk about anything . . ."

"Nope." Not talking about anything. "I'm good."

STAYING AWAY FROM THE CORNER STORE

Don't want to be anywhere near that shamrock.

Trying to shove Los Crooks out of my head. Easy to say. Harder to do.

Cut through an alley. Graffiti's everywhere. Need to get my name up. Look all around. Can of Juice Green out of my backpack. Nope. Los Crooks could make the connection. Silver Sharpie instead. Look again. Now.

ST. B

Yep. I'm here.

Head down the alley. "Whoa." Huge graffiti piece stops me dead in my tracks. It's the most beautiful thing I've ever seen. Covers the whole wall beside me.

Can't move. Can't look away.

Grabs me by the front of my shirt. Won't let me go. Screaming to be noticed.

Step forward. Touch it. Move my hand around the design. Pretend that I'm spray painting this. Take it all in. Shape of the outline. Design of the letters. Amazing colors. Reds. Blues. Greens. Yellows. Purples. Colors so incredible I can almost taste them.

Step back. "What is this?" I'm far enough away to see the whole thing. It's the size of a billboard. Huge bird flying out of ashes. A phoenix. The words RISE UP look like they're flowing under its wings. Pushing it to go up. Higher and higher.

Amazing graffiti masterpiece. Spray-painted in an alley. In my hood. Not hanging on the wall in a boojie museum. Out where everyone can see it. Touch it. Study it.

For free.

Need to learn how to create a piece like this. Then everyone will stare at my work. In awe. Inspired to think.

DIGGING THROUGH MY BACKPACK

Saint Al's crew-neck sweatshirt.

Black Sharpie.

Grape Bubble Yum wrappers.

Student ID.

Red spiral notebook.

Introduction to Latin.

Almost-empty can of Juice Green.

One sock.

Blackbook.

Silver Sharpie.

Empty wallet.

Gym shorts.

Rubber bands.

Metro Transit bus pass.

The Chocolate War.

Pull out my blackbook. The phoenix on my mind.

WALKING TO MOST HOLY TRINITY

Early morning. Our hood's already busy. People out doing their own thing. Standing. Talking. Reading. Texting.

"It's *embarrassing* to be walked to school every day," Fiona says.

Declan grabs my hand. "I like it, Liam."

We wait to cross at the light and then take a left at the next street. Corner boys are trying to get rid of their daily packages. Pot. Crack. Meth. Prescription drugs. Turn right. The corner market. Crap. Went this way by habit.

Big Juice Green shamrock's on the sidewall.

"Hey, that's cool." Patrick stops.

Fiona steps closer. "I think it's kind of pretty."

"Let's go." Motion for Declan. "You guys are going to be late for school."

"Awesome! Irish Mafia finally got the wall." Patrick lifts his fist. Waits for me to bump it. "Screw Los Crooks."

"Knock it off, Patrick."

"No, I'm repping Irish Mafia."

"No you're NOT." I grab his arm.

Owner comes out. "Hey, break it up. No trouble or I'm calling the cops." He points at me. "I know your mother."

"Come on." I shove Patrick. "Keep walking."

PASSING A GUY FROM THE JFKs

I'm walking down the hall at Saint Al's. The only other guy I know here from the projects walks toward me. He's a junior. I have to say something. "Hey."

He nods. "How's it going?"

"I'm good."

He motions toward the bathroom. "In here."

Drops his Crusaders basketball duffel bag on the floor. "Word around JFKs"—he checks under the stalls—"says you're marked."

"What?"

"On someone's shit list."

"No big deal." My stomach cramps.

"Damn. Are you stupid? Word is you tagged for Irish Mafia. Los Crooks are pissed. My brother was asking about you. His Bloods had that wall before Los Crooks."

Shrug. Can't believe this is happening. Now what?

"What are you doing, O'Malley? Playing baby banger?"

"I'm not in a gang."

"You tagged for one."

"That's only because my bro . . . Doesn't matter."

"Where we come from, *everything* matters. We've got to soldier on like every single damn decision matters."

"But I . . ."

"Shut the hell up. Quit throwing away your chance, man." He walks out the door.

DEBATING JOE MAUER'S CAREER

Me. Tyrell. Sean. Playing catch at the park. Our usual routine.

"Twins gave Mauer a 184-million-dollar contract for eight years. To catch." Tyrell is quoting numbers again. "He's too good to be on the bench."

Sean throws me a grounder. "He's not even on the bench, dude. He's on the disabled list."

"Your boy's hurt again." I point at Tyrell. "Second time this season."

"Then make him the DH, losers. The guy can hit."

"What!" Sean drops his glove. "You're crazy, Tyrell. Pay him that chunk of change to be the designated hitter?"

I clear my throat. "Now at DH for the Minnesota Twins, Joe Mauer, this year's 2.3-million-dollar benchwarmer." Try not to laugh.

Sean falls on the ground. Laughing so hard, he's crying.

"Okay, okay, I get it," Tyrell says. "Don't pee your pants."

"Hey, Liam." Sean picks his glove up. "How much is Saint Al's paying you to play baseball for them?"

"Would have been whatever tuition costs. I guess fifteen or twenty thousand."

"Liam O'Malley, the twenty-thousand-dollar shortstop

for the Saint Aloysius Gonzaga Crusaders." Tyrell laughs. "Still just a knucklehead from the hood."

I punch him. He punches me. Sean joins in. Where are the girls?

"Doesn't matter now anyway." Pick up the baseball. "I got cut." It's a lie.

"WHAT THE HELL?" Sean. "They recruited you."

"They didn't want a freshman. I'm not playing anymore." Actually, after what my teammates did, I just stopped going to practice. "No big deal." Hate Saint Al's.

SITTING IN MASS AT SCHOOL

My assigned pew is in the middle of the freshmen section. Headmaster stares at me. Priest gives the homily. His lecture. "We must remember that God is always with us. He never leaves us."

Yeah, right.

Where was God when Los Crooks saw me tagging? When Dad hit Mom? When Patrick's friend got shot because some guy wanted his bike?

Nowhere.

Same nonsense I hear every Sunday at our parish church.

"Everyone stand and join me in a most beloved hymn, 'Amazing Grace'."

No, thanks.

AVOIDING HIS EYES

Sitting in the headmaster's office. Apparently the dean doesn't want to deal with me anymore.

"I'm concerned, Mr. O'Malley." He folds his hands on top of the desk. "It appears as though your priorities are in the wrong place. We gave you a full scholarship to attend Saint Aloysius Gonzaga. We even provided you with free lunches."

Shrug.

"Why did you quit the baseball team, *son*?"

"Doesn't matter." Who's he calling son? "You wouldn't believe me if I told you."

"Have you completely forgotten that Saint Al's took a chance on you?"

Check my fingernails. I took a chance. It failed.

"You showed so much promise for a young man from an inner-city neighborhood."

"*Promise?*" Nothing's ever promised in the hood.

"Coach was convinced that you playing shortstop was the final piece to a state championship trophy. A real shame. We didn't have you tagged as a quitter."

Stare at the crucifix on the wall behind his desk. Don't know if I'll ever tell anyone why I quit the team.

"Your teachers tell me you're behind on your schoolwork. And you haven't shown much effort to try to join our Saint Al's community."

"So?"

"So, I fear that you're a train wreck waiting to happen, Mr. O'Malley."

PICKING UP AN ANTI-GRAFFITI BROCHURE

It's from a brand-new display case at the bus stop. Los Crooks already tagged the plexiglass.

Reading blah, blah, blah . . . "and no solution can be effective against the few individuals who may be determined to apply graffiti in spite of every effort to prevent them."

I mess around with these words in my blackbook.

I will apply graffiti in spite of every effort to prevent me.

Prevent me, and I am determined to apply graffiti.

I prevent every effort to spite graffiti.

Spite will apply graffiti—prevent me.

Apply graffiti in every effort.

Spite me, I apply graffiti.

Spite in every graffiti.

I apply spite graffiti.

Graffiti in me.

Graffiti.

Me.

Take graffiti away?

Like covering my mouth with duct tape.

WANDERING HOME FROM THE BUS STOP

JFKs are two blocks up ahead. Kids move around broken glass. Draw chalk houses on the sidewalk. Another day done at Saint Aloysius Gonzaga. Patron saint of teenagers. Yeah, right.

Only one more month of ninth grade. Then freedom for the whole summer.

Sneak past our projects' community garden. Mom and Mrs. Murphy cutting rhubarb. I'm supposed to help. Would rather sketch. Work on new tag designs.

Three guys dressed in black and silver turn the corner. Rosaries around their necks. They're Los Crooks.

I walk past them without looking.

"Who you bang with?" I hear.

Keep walking.

"Yo, schoolboy," someone shouts. "I'm talking to you."

Turn around. "Yeah, what's good?" Chest tightens.

He walks up to me. "I asked who you bang with, man." A black *LC* is tattooed across his neck.

"Nobody."

"You think I'm playing?" His fist slams my chest. "You're with Irish Mafia. What were you doing at the corner market three weeks ago?"

Holy crap. Tagging for Irish Mafia. "I don't remember," I lie.

He laughs. Gets up in my face. His breath smells like weed.

"Maybe this will help you." One of the other guys hands him a cell phone.

I'm done.

"Take a look." Los Crooks shoves the phone toward me. "Gotcha, youngin." Holds it two inches in front of my eyes. "Repping Irish Mafia."

Play dumb. "I don't know what you mean."

"You tagged over Los Crooks." Spit flies onto my face. "That's what I mean, pendejo!"

I can't breathe. Heart pounds under my Saint Al's logo.

"I don't bang."

"Don't lie to me, schoolboy. You know what I do to liars?" Lifts his shirt. Silver Glock handgun in his waistband.

"I'm not lying." Going to vomit. "I'm not Irish Mafia."

"He's dissing you," the guy on his right spits. "Represent Los Crooks, man. Put a cap in that clown."

My chin shakes. His left eye twitches.

The third Los Crooks whistles. "Po-po."

It's a black-and-white. Minneapolis Police cruise by. Only five feet away. Passenger window halfway down. Both cops look at us. I want to yell for help. Los Crooks will shoot me before the cop even slams it into park.

The Los Crooks with the neck tat puts his hand out toward me. Like he wants to shake. "Nice to see you, homie. Me and the boys will stop by to meet your family."

I could scream for help. Could try to punch him.

Instead I stick my hand out. Shake his. Cop sitting in the passenger seat turns away. No. Don't go. Don't leave me here with these guys. Black-and-white keeps rolling. Around the corner.

Los Crooks guy with the tat looks back at me. "You're smarter than I thought, junior. I got eyes all around. Know what I mean?" The other two Los Crooks throw down the hand sign for Irish Mafia.

Disrespecting my brother's gang. Testing me.

Need to get out of here. "Yeah," I say. And then I run. Get halfway down the block.

All three are on me in a second. Knock me to the sidewalk. Jerk me up by the collar. Gun grinds into my cheek.

"You're about to get a lesson in respect."

"Shoot him, man!"

Glock jabs against my forehead. "I'm gonna OFF you, fool."

"Please. No." I'm going to die right here on this sidewalk. Help me, God.

The third Los Crooks whistles again. Glock goes into the waistband. Are the cops back?

"Liam!" It's my mom's voice. She walks this way. Arms filled with rhubarb. "Get up off the ground in your school uniform. Use some common sense."

I get up. Fast. Try not to look scared. Did she see his gun?

"Come home and change before you get together with your friends." She walks past the Los Crooks guys. "Lord knows I don't have time to go to the Laundromat tonight."

Pull my backpack on. Los Crooks with the tat pulls me back.

Talks through clenched teeth. "I'll find where you live, man." Points to his eyes, then at me. "Get on home and do your schoolwork. Hail Mary and all that bullshit." He shoves me backward.

Mom turns. "Let's go, Liam. Right now!" Her eyes are huge.

Los Crooks taps the Glock in his waistband. "See you later. Friend."

Walk away. Whole body shaking.

"Yo!" One of the other bangers shouts down the block. "When you get home, you better check your drawers, fool. You pissed your pants!"

GENUFLECTING AT CHURCH

And it's not even Sunday. Extreme fear does that.

Sitting in our usual O'Malley family pew.

Habit.

Trying to figure out what happened yesterday. Need to quiet my mind. Sun shines through stained-glass windows. Across my face.

Had a Glock in my face.

Bend down. Onto the kneeler. Pull a prayer card out of my pocket. It's Saint Brendan the Navigator. My hands shake. But seeing his face calms me down. Walk over to the prayer candles.

Los Crooks were going to kill me.

Drop my quarter into the coin slot under the rows of twenty-four-hour votive candles. Light the long wooden match. Try to hold my hands still. Flame of my candle goes up. I kneel down. Cross myself.

"Keep me safe, God. Protect me from those bangers. Please help me know what to do."

What *am* I going to do?

BEING INTERRUPTED BY MOM

"You remember Kat."

"No." She got me my blackbook.

"Katherine Sullivan, my friend from Southie. You know, in Boston. She took us to Disney World when you kids were little. She came to visit us a few summers ago."

"Nope." Took me to the Walker Art Center. My favorite art museum. Contemporary.

"Oh, for the love of Jesus. The artist—she makes sculptures. You liked spending time with her."

"Umm. I'm not sure." Open *The Chocolate War*. Irritate Mom.

"Liam." Hands on her hips.

"Oh yeah. Right. Kat."

"Mom!" Fiona's in the kitchen. "Will you help me with this knife?"

"Oh, Lord, don't move!" Mom looks at me. "You either."

The Chocolate War. Book report due in three days. Chapter one: "They murdered him. As he turned to take the ball, a dam burst against the side of his head and a hand grenade shattered his stomach. Engulfed by nausea, he pitched toward . . ."

Mom interrupts. "Kat's invited you to stay with her in Michigan for the summer."

Back to the book "... he pitched toward the grass. His mouth encountered gravel, and he spat frantically, afraid that some of his teeth had been knocked out."

"You're interested in art, Liam. You can see how Kat works as an artist. You might learn something."

Look up from my page. She's not going to stop talking.

"Not interested." Check my fingernails.

"It's very thoughtful of her."

"No, thanks. Already have plans with Tyrell and Sean." Might even try to talk to that new girl. "I'm good right here."

"Actually—" she says. Then she changes her tone. "You're not."

Here we go.

"Things aren't good here. It's like you're on a shipwreck and you're not even trying to save yourself. Don't you think I know what's been going on at Saint Al's? The headmaster phoned me yesterday."

Something's about to happen. Heart races.

"A change of scenery would be good for you. Kat has a wonderful house on the beach of Lake Michigan. Lakeshore is a small town."

"What?"

"It's the perfect place for you to spend the summer. So you're going."

"No!" Fight or flight.

"I will not have another one of my sons running the

streets, doing God-knows-what, as a criminal. You're going, Liam. I won't lose another child to a gang."

"I'm not in a gang!"

"Then what was that the other day with those Los Crooks? You don't think I saw his gun?"

I didn't know what to think. "That wasn't a big deal," I say.

"No big *deal*? You have no idea, Liam." She starts to cry. "No idea whatsoever."

"Mom."

"No. I will not let you turn out like your brother. He's just like your . . ." She walks away.

"Just like Dad?"

She's back in my room. "You're leaving in two weeks."

"This isn't fair!"

I run. Out of the bedroom. The apartment. The JFKs.

I run until I can't breathe anymore.

REJOINING MY BASEBALL "COMMUNITY"

Hit the varsity team room. Home of the Saint Al Crusaders. Find my old locker. Empty. Smells like pee.

Look all around. Can of Juice Green out of my backpack.

CLIKCLAKCLIKCLAKCLIKCLAK.

Look again.

Now. *PSSSSSSSSSSSSSSSSSSSSSSSSST.* Cover the front of the locker.

ST. B
WAS HERE

Empty the can. Wrecking the perfect boojie paint job.

Listen.

I exist.

UNWINDING ON THE ROOF

Me. Tyrell. Sean. At the JFKs. Sitting in our Dumpster-dive lawn chairs. Twenty-six floors above the hood. Can touch the sky. Almost. Peaceful. Windows of the skyscrapers downtown light up the almost-dark sky. When I squint, the buildings look like Christmas trees.

"Can't believe school's out in two weeks." Tyrell lifts his arms up behind his head.

"Not for me, dudes." Sean throws a chunk of tar over the edge. "I have to do summer school."

"Again?" Tyrell laughs.

"It's not funny, loser. I can't get algebra clear in my head."

Silence.

"You guys see that new girl from Tower Four?" I whistle. "Amazing."

"Long black hair?" Tyrell smirks.

"That's the one."

Sean throws more tar. "Too bad her mom's a crackhead."

BANGBANGBANG!

The shots sound from right below us. Down on the street.

BANG! BANG!

"A thirty-eight?" Tyrell stands.

"No," Sean says. "Too fast. Maybe nine millimeter."

"You're right. A Glock." Tyrell nods. "Definitely a Glock."

They bump fists.

Glock? If these guys only knew what's been going on. Not saying a word. Too dangerous. Los Crooks have eyes all around. Can't put my family in danger. Don't want to worry my friends.

"When's Saint Al's done, Liam?" Sean kicks my chair.

"Next week. Hate that place."

"Who cares? Use them to get what you want." Tyrell shrugs. "If you graduate from Saint Al's, you can go to any college you want. Play the game, man."

"No. I couldn't care less about Saint Al's." I stand up. "Just found out my mom's sending me away for the summer."

"What do you mean? She can't do that." Sean spits. "Can she?"

"Yeah. She can. She's making me go to some crap town in Michigan."

"Damn, Liam." Tyrell punches my arm. "That's rough."

Don't even want to punch him back.

PULLING WEEDS

Mom always says, "You all like to eat? Then you all have to help in the garden."

So here I am. JFK community garden. O'Malley family plot. Move a row closer to Mom. "You don't have to send me to Michigan." Worth a try.

She ignores me.

I don't give up. "Then I guess I'll have to miss my confirmation classes."

"Kieran's didn't start until fall." She wipes dirt on her jeans. "October, I think. So you'll be back in plenty of time."

Great.

"I've got stuff to do. I'm signed up for the park baseball league. I'll stay out of trouble."

"I pray that you will." She crosses herself. "That you'll make some big changes in your life."

"I can do it here."

"No."

"*Mom.*"

"Stop, Liam. You need to be away from here. It's not safe for you. Especially hanging out with Kieran's gang."

"C'mon. I don't bang. Already told you that. I only did one tag for Irish Mafia."

"And that one tag almost got you shot."

Yeah. Stupid to trust Kieran. "I don't want to tag for gangs. I want to be a graffiti writer."

"Why would you put yourself in any danger because of graffiti? Maybe you should try to figure out why it's so important that you're willing to waste your life over it."

"*Waste my life?*"

Graffiti is my only way to show that I even *have* a life.

YELLING INTERRUPTS OUR GAME OF PEPPER

Me. Tyrell. Sean.

"Heyyy!" Getting louder. "Yo! LIAM!"

Look around. Where's it coming from?

"Irish Mafia's strolling this way," Sean warns. "Kieran, Tommy, another guy."

One of them falls. Loud laughter follows.

"Great." Tyrell lowers his voice. "I was hoping a bunch of drunk fools would show up here today."

"LIAM O'MAAALLEY! I'm looking for my bro. You here, man?"

"Crap." I look down at my fingernails.

"Liam!" Kieran sways.

Stare. Want to run.

Bangers stand in front of us. All three wearing green-and-white Boston Celtics jerseys. Shamrock tattoos on their left biceps.

Kieran steps closer. "I've been looking for you, bro." His breath stinks.

I remember that smell. "What do you want?"

"Need to talk to you." Points at Tyrell and Sean. "Alone."

"You heard him, kids." Tommy makes a fist. "Step off."

"No problem, dude." Sean throws up the hand sign for Irish Mafia.

Tyrell looks at me. "We've got your back, Liam."

Nod. "See you later."

"We need another taaaaaag, St. B." Kieran puts his arm over my shoulder.

Guy hands a bottle to Kieran. Irish whiskey. He takes a drink. Passes it on.

Tommy shoves it toward me. "Here, take a swig." Shamrock on the label.

Shake my head.

Kieran laughs. "Go ahead, take a drink, ya little girl."

Chest tightens. Exactly what Dad said to Kieran. I was five. Kieran was nine. He didn't want to. Dad said, "Take a damn drink, ya little girl." Kieran did as he was told. He started coughing and crying. Dad laughed. Made him drink more. Kieran and I promised each other that we'd never drink like him. We always promised. Even after Dad left.

"No, Kieran."

"Then don't take a drink, bro." He laughs. "Means more for me."

"I mean no, don't ask me to do any more tags for your gang."

"Who's in charge here, K-O?" Tommy jabs his knuckle into Kieran's tattoo. "Rep Irish Mafia. Teach this boy a lesson."

Kieran stares.

"C'mon, man." Tommy shoves him. "Step up or step off, K-O."

Kieran gets up in my face. "I'm not *asking*. I'm *telling*, junior."

"Hey," park security yells. He's walking this way. "Couple of kids told me there's some trouble over here."

Thank God. A security guy's actually in the park for once.

"No problem, man." Kieran backs off. "Just having a conversation with my brother."

"Not anymore." Security won't let Kieran mess with me.

I walk around Irish Mafia. "I'm leaving."

GETTING KICKED TO
THE CURB

Welcome to Minneapolis–St. Paul International Airport.

Mom swerves the church's turd-brown minivan into an open space. Departure area. The little kids are in the back seat. They ramble on about the airport. Patrick sits in the way back.

Signs warn: "No stopping allowed. If you see suspicious activity, call 911." Suspicious activity? See something? Say something? Yeah, right. That makes you a punk where I come from.

"Please, please, please. Can we please go into the airport?" Fiona begs.

Declan joins in. "Please, please, please. Liam wants us to, Mommy."

"We can't." She's pulling things out of her purse. "We don't have time."

I get out. Sit down on my Crusaders baseball duffel bag. Look around. People hug. Cry. Shake hands good-bye. Is anyone else being sent away for the summer?

Fiona presses her forehead against the window. "Come on. Let's see the inside."

Third time I've been here. Once when we flew to Disney

World with Kat. The other when we flew to Southie for Uncle Danny's funeral. I was six. Mom was pregnant with Fiona. Dad told us, "I hated that son of a bitch." He stayed home.

"Yeah, so Liam's not lonely," Declan says.

"Not right now." Mom leans under the dashboard. "I'm trying to find something,"

Airport rent-a-cop stares at me. This area is for curbside loading and unloading only.

"Hey, what's that cop doing?" Fiona points.

"Police officer," Mom corrects her. "Liam, are you sure I didn't give you that envelope?"

"I'm sure."

Cop slaps the side of the minivan. Mom's head flies up and hits the rearview mirror. "This is for drop-off only, ma'am. Keep it moving."

"Liam, check your duffel bag."

"No envelope, Mom."

"Let's go into the airport! Let's go into the airport!" Fiona and Declan are chanting now. Jumping on the seat. Minivan's bouncing up and down like the lowriders around our hood.

"JESUS, MARY, AND JOSEPH." Mom glares at the little kids. "Knock it off, you two. I can't even hear myself think. Shite."

Silence.

Then Fiona whistles. "That's a bad word, Mom."

"Uh-oh." Declan crosses himself. "Mrs. A. said that it makes baby Jesus cry in heaven when someone uses the Lord's name in vain."

"Great." Fiona puts her hands on her head. "Now you might have to go to hell when you die."

Declan starts to cry. "I don't want you to go to hell, Mommy."

"I'm not going to hell. I didn't use the Lord's name in vain. Zip your lips."

They do.

"Found it." Mom jumps out of the minivan. Runs around to me. "Give this to Kat when you get to the airport. It's your medical papers, a copy of your birth certificate . . ."

"Okay."

"She's meeting you at the luggage area."

"I know."

"You remember what she looks like?"

"I guess."

"Are you sure? It's been a few years."

"Yes."

Fiona pounds on the window. Making faces. Declan looks at me. Tears on his cheeks.

"Okay." Mom wipes the sweat off her face. "You've got everything, right?"

"This isn't fair."

"I cannot do this right now. We've already talked about all of this."

"Actually, Mom, we didn't talk about all of this. YOU told me what your plan was for MY summer."

"Let's go." Cop lifts his walkie-talkie. "This is your last warning, lady."

Want to scream. Why don't you go to south Minneapolis, where you're actually needed, you piece of crap? Go to my hood, where there's always "suspicious activity."

"Okay. We've got to go." Mom's hugging me. "I love you, Liam."

"Really?" Don't send me away. Please.

"Send us some postcards," Fiona says. Declan presses his face against the window. Patrick stares straight ahead.

Mom's eyes fill with tears. "This will be a good thing."

Feel like a balloon that all the air just went out of.

She gets back in the minivan. Grinds it into gear. Leans toward the passenger window. "See you in three months, Liam."

Shite. I give a pathetic wave to the little kids.

REPEATING SAINT BRENDAN'S WORDS

I say them in my head.

I fear that I shall journey alone, that the way will be dark;
I fear the unknown land, the presence of my King and the
sentence of my judge.

Chose Saint Brendan as my saint for First Communion. He was Irish. He loved the water. He questioned God. I've had his holy medal around my neck since I was seven. Never take it off.

Now I fear the unknown. "Saint Brendan, pray for me."

FLYING TO LAKESHORE, MICHIGAN

Turbulence most of the way. Figures. Sketch in my black-book. Try not to think about Minneapolis. Design some new letter styles that are like that very cool masterpiece in the alley.

Gliding over a huge lake. More like an ocean. Nothing but water down there.

Lake Michigan.

So many shades of blue. Sometimes light. Sometimes dark. Always changing.

The loudspeaker turns on. "Ladies and gentlemen, we are now flying over the western shore of northern Michigan. The captain has turned the seat belt signs back on. We are in our final descent and will be landing shortly."

Northern Michigan? Lots of trees and sand. No big city. No skyscrapers. No project towers. Nothing but huge empty spaces.

All summer.

Big sand cliffs. Big beach. Small town.

Crap.

ARRIVING FOR MY SUMMER GETAWAY

Baggage claim. Woman holds a sign with *O'Malley* written on the front. She's about my size.

Katherine Sullivan. Mom's best friend. My guardian for the entire summer.

She's smiling my way. Just like I remember. I smile back.

No.

Straighten my mouth. Back to my street scowl. Don't want her to know I'm nervous. Show no weakness, O'Malley.

She's walking toward me in a cool, inspired sort of way. Purposeful. Scuffed brown cowboy boots.

"Welcome to Michigan, Liam." Hugs me like she means it.

"Thanks."

She looks at me. "I knew it was you straightaway, even though it's been a while. What, two or three years at least?"

"Yeah."

"And I kind of cheated. Your mom sent me a photo."

"She likes to send those." I'm an idiot. Quit talking.

"Your eyes are older."

Shrug.

"So you had a good flight?"

"Yeah. It was fine."

"How about Lake Michigan?"

"Looks like an ocean."

"I love the big lake. It's the main reason I live here." The luggage carousel clunks and begins moving. "So, you've got a suitcase or something, right?"

"Yeah, I've got baggage."

RIDING SHOTGUN

Kat's gray Range Rover is old. But cool. No bumpers, but there's a sticker on the back that reads *Start seeing sculpture.*

Driving past forests. Farms. Trailer houses with junk in their front yards. Cars up on cement blocks. Reminds me of home.

"About five more minutes until we get to my house." Kat smiles.

"Okay." Things look nicer the closer we get to town. Completely opposite of home, where the hood can be junky and the burbs are taken care of.

"Look straight ahead," she says.

I see a huge white concrete post in the shape of a lighthouse. *Welcome to Lakeshore!* is painted down the front in red letters.

"Oh." I'm going to be *here* for the whole summer? My stomach feels like a bowl of rice all clumped together. Thanks a lot, Mom.

"So this is the east end of downtown." Kat points.

"Nice," I lie, because it looks boring. I want to go home.

"I'll drive slowly so you can get a good look."

No need. "Sure." Could hit a baseball from one end to the other.

Charter fishing place. Moped rental. Restaurants that serve burgers and fries. Fudge store. Bars. Kayak rental. Ice-cream place. Stores selling sweatshirts with lighthouses on the front. Lakeshore Town Hall. Old church with a tall steeple. Taller than everything else. Hardware store. Movie theater. Shows only Sunday through Thursday at eight? Great. What do people even do on the weekends here?

"Lake Michigan's straight ahead. And there's the light-house." She points again.

"Oh." Lighthouse. Of course.

"A beam of light from the lighthouse shines in the windows of my house when there's fog or a storm."

"Hmmm."

"Anyway. I live three blocks over, on the beach."

"The beach?"

TURNING ONTO A NARROW STREET

Blowing sand swirls around. We pull into the yard. Well, onto the yard. Not a parking lot. Not a concrete driveway. Hard-packed dirt with no grass. Kat parks the Rover.

She sighs. "Home sweet home."

"Hmmm." To her, maybe.

"Been here for the last twelve years," she says. "I moved here from New York. I needed to get out of the city. I lived in bigger cities my whole life. From growing up in Southie, in the projects with your mom, to New Haven, Connecticut, for art school, to NYC, to this little town. It suits me."

She talks a lot. "Oh."

Get out of the Rover. Try to take everything in. Yellow house with three floors. Five apartments in the JFKs would fit into Kat's house. Mom and the little kids would like this. Patrick, too.

Not me. It's not home.

Another smaller building off to the right. Windows all around.

"That's my studio."

"Studio?" Right. An artist.

"Where I work on my sculptures—and my pottery."

"Oh." Very cool.

"Mostly I'm a high-school art teacher at the academy up the coast.

Nod.

"So, I'm starving. What about you?"

"A little." Could eat a whole Thanksgiving dinner.

"Let's go in and see what we can find. Your mom let me know what your favorite foods are, so I stocked up. You should've seen the woman at the co-op when I piled all the ramen on the counter."

"You didn't have to get special stuff."

"No problem. I may even eat some of the ramen. I lived on it when I was in graduate school."

Grab my backpack and Crusaders duffel bag. Hear the waves from Lake Michigan as we walk toward the house.

Definitely not in the hood anymore.

WAITING FOR THE SUN TO SET

The front porch of Kat's house looks out onto the beach. A sandy front yard with clumps of tall grass all around. It slopes down a little hill to the beach. Lake Michigan's straight out. A baseball field away. This is actually pretty decent.

Screen door creaks open.

"This is my favorite time of day." Kat sits down. "I love watching the sun disappear into the big lake. Seeing different neighbors walk past on their way down to the beach. Everybody knows everybody. It's nice to say hi."

Sunset in the projects means something completely different. Around the JFKs we already know the people who are out on the streets after dark. See them heading home when I walk Patrick, Fiona, and Declan to Most Holy Trinity each morning. Sister Therese gathers the empty bottles, needles, used condoms from the playground. Tells us, "God has given us another beautiful day."

Yeah, right.

"There it goes." Kat points at the sun.

And then the huge ball of fire sinks into the water.

BEGINNING MY DETENTION

First full day in Lakeshore.

Stay in bed as long as I want. No Mom telling me to get up and take the garbage down to the smelly Dumpster. That's the second okay thing about being in Lakeshore. It's quiet here, too. Nothing but the sound of waves.

Stomach growls like an angry dog. Time to get up. Saint Al's Crusaders shorts on. Down the stairs.

Kat's sitting at the table. Paintbrush stuck behind her ear. "Good morning, Liam."

"Morning."

She has a ceramic mug the color of Lake Michigan in her hands. Lifts it toward me. "My get-up-and-go."

"Oh." I nod. Not sure what to do next.

"Breakfast?" She's wearing a faded Yale Fine Arts T-shirt.

"Sure."

"There are bagels from the bakery and fruit from the farmers market in the kitchen." She says. "Help yourself. *Domus mea domus tu est.*"

Latin. My house is your house. Is she testing me?

"*Gratias tibi ago.*" Thank you.

She laughs. "Chalk one up for Catholic-school education."

Walk into the kitchen. Get a bagel. And another. Since it's my house.

"I've got to drive up to the arts academy. There's a summer camp staff meeting."

"Okay." Strawberry juice runs down my chin. Need to slow down.

"Feel free to go down to the beach. Check out our little town if you want. Or just relax and do nothing."

"Cool." Detention? Maybe freedom is more like it.

After Kat leaves I notice a slip of paper on her fridge. It reads:

"I am for an art that is political-erotical-mystical, that does something other than sit on its ass in a museum." (Claes Oldenburg)

Huh?

Oh . . . I get it. Ha.

Wait.

What?

GAZING AT THE ROLLING WAVES

Lake Michigan is amazing. Like an ocean.

It's early afternoon. Have almost the whole beach to myself. Weird to be sitting here after being in Minneapolis only yesterday. Sand falls through my fingers like it would inside one of those glass things that shows the passing of time.

Mom sending me to Lakeshore for the summer was not okay. Still.

Water.

Waves.

Everything looks, sounds, feels, smells, tastes different from home. Maybe I could get used to this.

Nothing around me but water. And sand. And trees on the cliff. Seagulls overhead. People mind their own business. No need to hope someone's covering my back. Peaceful.

But it's not home.

Not going to buy into all of this straightaway. I'm from the hood. No one better try to take that away from me. My identity belongs to me. And no matter where I am, or where I have to be, I'm not necessarily what's around me. May have to be a part of my surroundings, but I can be separate from them. What stays inside is everything that's ever happened to me.

Don't expect me to change.

RECEIVING A CALL

"It's your mom," Kat says.

Maybe she changed her mind. Probably wants me to come home.

"Hello?"

"I just got off the phone with your headmaster." She sounds irritated.

"Oh." Walk out to the front porch.

"Well, that's quite a response. Don't you want to know why he called me?"

"I guess." Not really.

"You *guess*? Why don't you take a guess, then, Liam?"

"Ummm. I'm not sure."

She lets out a huge sigh. "He told me they made every effort to help you get on the right path but that you refused to meet them even partway. Mentioned something about defacing school property. He said they waited until after the end of the year in hopes that you'd turn it around."

"What're you talking about?"

"Liam, they've made the decision not to let you come back to Saint Al's next year."

"What?" Hate Saint Al's. But can't believe they kicked me out.

"They're pulling your scholarship and giving it to another student-athlete who can more fully appreciate it."

"They recruited me. This isn't fair."

"What's not fair? I'm told you stopped showing up to practice. And you've only got yourself to blame for your behavior."

"*My* behavior?" What about the behavior of my teammates? This is because I quit baseball. Who cares? I'm glad.

"Now you've gotten kicked out of a good school. Maybe someday you'll learn that you just have to . . . GOD DAMMIT, Liam. You have to at least *try*."

Never hear her use the Lord's name in vain.

Wow.

THINKING ABOUT SAINT AL'S

Termination.

Irritation.

Humiliation.

Satisfaction?

Miseducation.

Incarceration.

Disconfirmation.

Elimination.

Retaliation?

Contemplation.

TURNING TO A CLEAN PAGE

Need to draw in my blackbook. Try to piece together what's been happening.

Gun rammed against my head. Sent away for the whole summer. Kicked out of Saint Al's forever. Now where will I go to school? Nothing makes sense.

Practice my lettering. Come up with new ideas. What do I want to say? Nothing happens around here. Lakeshore, Michigan, is probably the most boring town in America. I'd have so many ideas if I were still at home. Always something going on. Nothing you can't do in Minneapolis.

Think of home. Remember being stretched out on my top bunk. Feet propped up on my pile of undone homework. Blackbook open. Messing around with different designs and colors. Trying to figure out my style.

Remembering back to the night before I left. Patrick on the bottom bunk. Schoolbooks open.

"Hey, Liam, when you read *The Giver* in seventh grade, did you have to do this future-community thing?" he asked.

"Everyone at MHT has to." Loved that project. "It was decent. I got to draw the design of the city for my group. Got an A."

"Would you draw me an idea for the layout of the city?" Patrick said.

"Aren't you supposed to?"

"Help me out, Liam."

"I'm busy right now." Wanted to do my own thing.

He sighed loud to make sure I heard him.

I hung my head over the side of my bed. "Why don't we work on it together?"

"Seriously?" He had a huge smile.

Made me feel good. "Yeah." Hoped that I'd have some more time to myself later.

Now, sitting here at Kat's, I've got all the solitude I've ever wanted. But I don't like it. Don't want time to think about all that crap.

Close my blackbook.

RELAXING AFTER DINNER

Usual routine. Same thing every night since I got here a week ago. Kat and I read, play board games, shoot the breeze a little. Never too much talking.

She's reading the *New York Times.* "No! Red Sox lost to the Yankees in extra innings."

"You're a Boston fan?"

"Since I could talk."

"Just like my mom."

"Absolutely. She and I used to skip school sometimes and sneak into Fenway Park to catch matinee games."

Laugh. Can't imagine Mom doing anything bad. "Did the Twins play yesterday?" I say.

"Let's see . . . Minnesota beat Chicago."

"Cool." I hate the White Sox. "Now I think we're only three games behind them in the standings. Just wait until Boston plays in Minneapolis."

"Bring it." Kat smiles. "Red Sox Nation!"

"Okay." Awkward.

Stretched out on the couch. Looking around the living room. Paintings. Photos. Couple of sculptures. Tons of books. No television. Very cool fireplace made of huge rocks. Can't imagine hauling them in from Lake Michigan, trying to make each one fit into just the right place. Like pieces in a puzzle.

Whole wall of books. I get up to take a closer look. They're mostly about art—or artists. Paul Gauguin. Joan Mitchell. Frida Kahlo. Keith Haring. Cy Twombly. I've seen something from most of these artists at the Walker Art Center back home. I've seen surrealists like Salvador Dalí there, too. Kat has a book about American women sculptors. One about Jackson Pollock and another on abstract art. Very cool. Pull a book about cubism off the shelf. Maybe she has something about Picasso. Vincent van Gogh. Jean-Michel Basquiat.

"Baskweeat?"

"Baz-KEE-ah. One of my favorite artists," Kat says. "You might like his work."

"Hmmm." Take the Basquiat book, too. It has a painting of a black angel on the cover. Surrounded by bright reds and oranges. Black-and-white photo of Basquiat on the back. Sitting on an old-fashioned chair. Like a king's throne. Wearing trousers with paint stains. Checkered suit coat. White shirt. Tie. Dreads pulled together like a waterfall on top of his head. Rests his chin on his left hand. Stares into the camera. Right at me. Sad look on his face. Like he's worn out.

Open the book. Amazing. Pages filled with bright yellows. Blues. Reds. Greens. Stick people like Declan draws. Words.

Images. Things scratched out. Names. Lists. Urban scenes. Familiar scenes. Says Jean-Michel Basquiat started out as a graffiti writer.

He was "driven by an insatiable hunger for recognition, fame and money, wavering between megalomania and an insurmountable shyness, plagued by self-doubt and self-destructive impulses." He died "of an overdose on August 12, 1988, aged just twenty-seven."

Self-destructive impulses?

His paintings are very cool. Why doesn't he look like he knows it?

WAKING UP IN MY SUMMER BEDROOM

Not the one I share with Patrick and Declan.

I sleep by a window overlooking Lake Michigan. Not by the one that opens onto a parking lot.

I'm in a room on the second floor of a house on a beach. Not in the one on the eleventh floor of a project in a big city.

Like night and day.

Grab my blackbook. My pencils. Hit the page. Try to capture this scene outside my window. No one would believe how phenomenal this is. Maybe I could turn this into a huge graffiti piece that would make people stop and stare. Just like my favorite phoenix piece. Maybe I can learn how to create something beautiful for everyone to enjoy in my hood.

I use colored pencils to show the tones of the lake. Fill the page with three different shades of blue. Turquoise for the small rolling waves up by the shore. Blue-green ripples farther out. Midnight blue where the big sailboats travel.

Copying what's around me.

Don't ever want to forget this scene.

SEARCHING FOR THE MEANING

Looking around the living room. Want to figure out those descriptions of Basquiat. Dreamed about him all night. Nightmares. His paintings came to life and were trying to beat the crap out of me. Chased me all around my hood. Screamed at me to stop. Basquiat just kept laughing. Then he started crying.

"Good morning." Kat walks down the stairs. "You're up early."

"Morning. Do you have a dictionary?"

"Over there." Points to the other side of the room. "On the shelf behind my desk."

"Thanks."

"Did you eat yet?"

"No, but I'll get something in a minute." Open the dictionary. Search through the M section.

Megalomania is "the enjoyment of having power over other people and the craving for more of it. A psychiatric disorder in which the patient experiences delusions of great power and importance."

Okay.

Think I know the definition of the other word. Want to be sure.

"*Insurmountable:* impossible to overcome or deal with successfully."

Basquiat loved power but didn't know how to deal with it? Maybe I should try to find out more about this artist.

Maybe not.

KNOCKING ON THE DOOR TO KAT'S STUDIO

Dying to see inside this place. Been looking through the windows when she's not around. Never actually asked to go in. Knock.

"Yes?"

"It's me, Liam."

"Come on in."

Kat's standing in the middle of the room. She's staring at some sort of sculpture made of shiny metal. Lifts a pair of goggles off her eyes. "Thanks for knocking, but this studio is always open to you. Okay?"

"Sure." This must be what artists' heaven looks like. Sun shining through the windows. Beams of light everywhere. Like an abstract painting. Concrete floor with big paint stains. Hunks of clay under a pottery wheel in one corner. Old stone fireplace covering one wall from the floor to the ceiling. Try not to smile. It's like someone asked me what my dream place would look like, saw it in my mind, then made it right here.

Sweet.

"Does it pass the test?"

Shrug. With flying colors. Walk over to a big wooden

table. Loaded with ceramic bowls. Pick one up. "What are all these?"

"My Lakeshore Empty Bowls Project."

"What?"

"One of my very favorite art projects. I make the bowls, the residents of the assisted living home decorate them, and women from Saint Catherine's parish use them to feed the hungry." She smiles. "I love everything about them."

"Oh." Put the bowl down. Don't want to drop it. Walk around the studio.

"Speaking of favorite projects, Liam, are you still working on your wonderful sketches?"

"Yeah."

"Good. What kinds?"

"Mostly graffiti."

"Hmmm." She nods.

"I want to be a graffiti writer."

"I love the intensity of that art form. But why exactly is the graffiti artist called a writer?"

"Because it means someone who practices the art of graffiti. Studies. Always trying to get better."

"You're a student, then."

"I'm just getting started." Too much talking.

"What forms?"

Maybe she knows what I'm talking about. "Tagging mostly."

"A tag is the graffiti artist's name right?"

"Yes."

She nods. "When did you become really interested in tagging?"

Probably safe to tell her. "Been bombing around my neighborhood for a couple of months."

"Bombing?"

"Getting my tag up. Quick and undercover. Bombing."

"Sounds mysterious. Tag names are secret, right?"

I nod.

"I'm intrigued by graffiti. Why do you like it?"

"Why not?"

She nods. "Fair enough."

"Any around here?"

"No." She laughs. "Graffiti shouted from everywhere in my Brooklyn neighborhood. Tags and, um, what are the big colorful graffiti paintings called?"

"Pieces. That's short for masterpieces." Glad I know my terms.

"Thanks. Pieces were all over NYC."

"They're everywhere in my hood, too."

"Some were quite intricate and beautiful," she says.

"There's this one in an alley by our projects that's so cool, I swear it should be on a gallery wall at the Walker."

"What makes it so appealing to you?"

I think for a second. "I don't know. It's different from other pieces I've seen. More professional."

"Do you find the graffiti work of others inspiring?"

I nod.

"I suppose it's like studying the masters in any other art form," she says.

"Sure."

Nice! Kat just called graffiti an art form.

NOTICING A SWINGING BOTTLE

A man in front of me holds it. He's wearing shorts covered with little anchors. Walking down the cereal aisle at the grocery store. That preppy look would last about ten seconds around the JFKs.

Kat stops in the middle of the aisle. "What kind of cereal do you like?"

"Cocoa Puffs are good." I've seen that kind of bottle before. Whiskey.

"So we'll get Cocoa Puffs and . . . Where is it? My favorite, Trix." She pulls a giant-size box off the shelf. "Silly rabbit."

"What?" My mind's suddenly on that night with Kieran.

"Oh, never mind." She puts the boxes into the cart with the organic milk, organic eggs, and organic all-natural cola.

We walk up and down the other aisles. Filling the cart to the top.

Now the guy with the bottle is standing in front of us in the checkout lane. I watch the bottle move on the conveyor belt. Big green shamrock on the label.

Irish Mafia.

Can't catch my breath. Like someone's standing on my chest. Why is this happening now? Shake my head. Come on. It's just a shamrock.

Thinking of Los Crooks. Whole body shakes. Light-headed. Had a silver Glock against my head.

My legs are wobbly. Hard to stay standing. Guess remembering is worse in this quiet town.

STANDING IN THE MIRROR

Staring at a stranger.

Does God see the person he hoped I'd be? Or does he see "a big disappointment," like everyone at Saint Al's said? Maybe both.

Who cares?

Where was God when that Los Crooks almost killed me? And how about when Kieran left me to do his dirty work for Irish Mafia? Maybe God has given up on me. Just like everyone else. Too much thinking.

My brain hurts.

GOING AROUND AN OLD MAN

It's a new day. I'm on my way to the hardware store on Main Street. List of supplies for Kat in my pocket. The old man in front of me is using a brown wooden cane, wearing a blue-and-gold Lakeshore Sailors football jacket. Can't keep walking this slow. Veer out to the left. Pass him.

"What's your hurry?"

Talking to me?

"Young people always in a hurry. Need to slow down. Stop and smell the roses now and then."

Great, Mr. Philosopher.

Put some distance between me and him. Who does he think he is? Talking to me like you know me, old man. I get some room. Breathing space. Don't need to have someone up in my face. Turn the other cheek and all that. Walk. Get to the hardware store. It's not open yet. Should have opened five minutes ago. Start clipping my fingernails. Mr. Philosopher walks toward me. Great. Pulls a wad of keys out of his pocket. Looks at me. I pretend to read the list from Kat.

"In a big hurry and you still had to wait, eh?"

Because you're late. I stare.

"Give me a minute to get the store opened up, then I'll let you in."

Ignore him.

Ten minutes later he walks back out without the jacket. Wears a plaid shirt and a gray sweater vest. It's summer. "Go on inside, gather those rakes, and bring them back out here." He points to the empty wall.

What did he just say? "Excuse me?"

"Give me a hand with the rakes, will ya?"

I follow him into the store. Gather eleven rakes. Carry them outside. Lean them against the front wall. Done.

"Now, give me a hand with these bags of fertilizer. They've got to be stacked in piles five high, starting here and going to here." He walks off a space about six feet long. "Got it?"

That means thirty bags? "Fine."

"Now take your time. Nice and straight or they'll fall over. No need to be in a hurry."

What the . . . ?

"When you're done come on inside and let me know what you need." He goes back into the store.

Forget that. What I need is to walk away from this crazy old man. I'm not doing this guy's job. I want to leave.

But I don't. These things are so heavy, I can only lift one at a time. This'll take forever. Got things to do. Yeah, right. Like what?

Finish my job. Head back into Mr. Philosopher's store.

"All right, then." He claps his hands. "What can I help you with this morning?"

Good question, since I've already helped him. Hand him Kat's list without saying a word.

"Okay. This way, young fella."

After about ten minutes we pile tubes of paint, wire netting, a container of turpentine, an aluminum bucket, drop cloth, wire brush, and one hundred feet of clothesline on the counter.

"Are you an artist?"

"It's for someone else."

"Who?"

"What?"

"Who's the someone else?" He scratches his bald head.

"Why?"

"I know most everybody around these parts."

"Kat, uh, Katherine Sullivan."

"The Lady Artist. I didn't know she had an assistant."

"She doesn't." Mind your own business. "I'm staying with her for the summer." Way too much talking.

"Where're you from?"

"Minneapolis."

"City boy, huh?"

He's really bugging me. "Yeah."

"We do things a lot differently here in Lakeshore. This being a small town and all."

Shrug. That's too bad.

"You'll get used to it." He nods.

No way.

"Clarence Masterson." Puts his hand out. "Folks around here just call me Hank."

Hank? How do you get that from Clarence?

"Liam O'Malley." We shake.

"They say you can judge the character of a man by his handshake." He looks at me without blinking.

I look back. Set a can onto the counter.

"Spray paint. Are you eighteen?"

I lie. "It's for Kat."

DECIDING TO WASTE MY LIFE AGAIN

Last night I remembered Hank's words. Small town, huh?

We do things a lot differently in the hood. Minneapolis being a big city and all.

Welcome to Lakeshore! I decide to offer my own kind of welcome.

I wake up extra early this morning. Need to get my artistic introduction done and be back to Kat's before sunrise.

Time to put my graffiti science in motion.

Look all around. Can of Midnight Black out of my backpack.

CLIKCLAKCLIKCLAKCLIKCLAK.

Check again.

Now. *PSSSSSSSSSSSSSSSSSSSSSSSSSST.* Paint invades the surface.

ST. B

Use the new handstyle I've been practicing in my blackbook. It's my own usual graffiti handwriting but more intricate and involved now. Need to keep changing things up if I want to get better as a writer.

Time to wake up this boring town.

I am here, Lakeshore. A bench and a garbage can prove it.

I exist.

SETTLING DOWN

Swimming in Lake Michigan. Trying to move slow and steady. Back and forth. My whole body feels like an electrical current. Slow down. Take a deep breath. Just me and the water.

I feel shaky all over. That was the second time I've tagged out of spite. The first time was my baseball locker at Saint Al's.

Stupid.

That's not what I want to do with my graffiti. I'm frustrated by everything that's been happening. I'm tired of always being angry.

Water's freezing. Cooling me down. Not so bad as long as I keep swimming. My arms are rubbery, but I'm not going to quit. The big lake will not beat me.

Crap. I'm exhausted.

Get back to shore. Solid ground.

"Liam?" It's Mom.

"Hi."

Chaos on the other end. Television blaring. Little kids arguing. Probably about what cartoon to watch.

"Be quiet, you two! I can't hear your brother." Declan starts crying. "Hang on a minute. I'll be right back. Patrick wants to talk."

"Hey, Liam," Patrick says.

"How's it going?"

"I've got to tell you something." He lowers his voice. "About Kieran."

"What?"

"You know Irish Mafia and Los Crooks hate each other. Now they're fighting over the same territory."

"So?" I say.

"So they got into it a couple nights ago."

"Kieran, too?"

"Yeah. Him, another Irish Mafia, that Los Crooks guy with the LC tattoo on his neck, and another Los Crooks."

"Holy crap."

"I know. Los Crooks were tagging over that big shamrock on the corner store. Irish Mafia stepped up. Kieran and the tattooed Los Crooks were both strapped, and they pulled their guns."

"Swear?"

"Yeah."

"Where'd Kieran get the gun?"

"Tommy. A Glock." Patrick pauses. "Oh, great, Mom's walking this way. I'm not supposed to know what happened. She has her hands on her hips. I have to go, Liam."

"Did he shoot one of the Los Crooks?"

"What did he tell you?" Mom raises her voice. "What did you tell him, Patrick?"

Patrick mumbles. Front door slams.

"This is nothing for you to be concerned about, Liam."

"What do you mean?"

"Kieran is making very poor choices, and now he has to deal with the consequences. That's it. How's Michigan?"

She always acts like everything's fine when she knows that I know it's not.

"What did Kieran do?"

Silence.

"Did he shoot someone?"

"Liam . . ."

"C'mon. I want to know what happened."

"Kieran and one of the Los Crooks were arrested. Your brother's in jail downtown until his arraignment."

"For what?"

"Using a firearm as a terroristic threat in the first degree, which means it was intentional. And the crime was committed for the benefit of a gang, which is a felony. That's all I know."

Wish I felt shocked. Don't. Not sure what I'm feeling.

"Liam?"

"What?"

"Your brother is eighteen. An adult. He's making his own decisions about how he wants to live his life. I hope that you're paying attention."

TREKKING TOWARD THE STEEPLE

Just like every Sunday morning at home. When Mom, Patrick, Fiona, Declan, and I walk five blocks from the JFKs to our parish church. For Mass. Past the corner boys in XXL white T-shirts and baggy shorts. Women dressed in as little as possible. The homeless pushing shopping carts that hold everything they own.

Every Sunday we sit in the front pew on the left side. Mom gives ten percent of her two-job income for the upkeep of the parish facilities. Meaning the priests' big houses in the burbs. While we're crowded in our two-bedroom apartment. We live in the hood, where the priests rarely drive their Cadillacs and Beemers. Where the nuns cram into the turd-brown minivan, gathering used clothes for the poor on our block. Always bless myself with holy water. Genuflect. Stand. Kneel. Reflect. Listen. Sing. Receive the body and blood of Christ. Amen.

It's where I have my doubts, like Saint Brendan did. But always keep my mouth shut. Like an obedient Catholic boy.

I reach Saint Catherine's Church. The tall steeple in Lakeshore.

Walk in. Red, yellow, and green votive candles line the

grotto. I move to touch the thin lit stick to the flame. No. Pull it back. Before the wick starts burning. Why should I light a prayer candle for Kieran?

Why does he deserve help? He's an adult. Like Mom said. He's making his own bad decisions. Only two green, one red, and two yellow candle holders left. Kieran covered his own back. Forgot about me even though I'm family. Shouldn't be concerned about him.

Light a red votive.

OBEYING MY NOSE

Walked past this bakery for days. Kat told me to explore Lakeshore. Said this little town can be quite inspiring to artists. Well, I did change the design of my tag since I've been here. Maybe she's right.

Keep seeing this bakery. Always want to go in. Something smells so good right now. Screen door creaks just like Kat's.

Look all around this bright-green place. Glass display on one side holds all of the reasons I wanted to come in.

Everything's set up on shelves like artwork. Little baked sculptures with name tags written in fancy handwriting.

White Coconut Cake

Raspberry Rhubarb Scones

Pumpkin Bread with Raisins

Blueberry Lemon Bread

Chocolate and Lavender Cupcakes

Cinnamon Rolls

Lemon Poppy Seed Muffins

I'll take one of everything.

"Can I help you?" a girl says.

"Ah. Ummm. I'm just looking."

"Well, do you have any questions?" Smiles. Brown hair pulled back into one of those fancy braids. She's probably my age.

"Trying to decide what looks the best," I say. She's even more beautiful than that girl from the JFKs.

"There's a larger bread selection over here."

Follow her over to another display case. Like a little puppy. I'd follow her anywhere.

"We've got spinach feta, pumpkin swirl, white cheddar garlic, artichoke parmesan, whole wheat, and classic white today."

What did she just say? "Okay."

Silence. Awkward.

"How about a sample?"

"What?" I'm an idiot.

"*Hello*. A sample. One of the breads or something?"

Definitely smiling at me. Is she checking me out? Because I sure am looking her over. Focus on the breads, O'Malley. Come up with something. "Sure, how about a piece of that huge cinnamon roll?"

She cuts a chunk off. Hands it to me.

"I'm Sara."

"Liam." Our fingers touch. "Thanks." Does she know I'm sweating bullets?

"Are you here on vacation?"

"Yeah." Look up at a painting of a lighthouse on the wall. So she won't think I'm staring at her. Lighthouses all over this town.

"I thought so. I've never seen you around here before." She touches her braid.

"Yeah." Silence. "Ah . . . I'm staying here for the summer. With a woman who's a friend of my mom's." Way too much talking.

"Anyone I know?"

"Who do you know?" What kind of pathetic question is that, O'Malley?

"Lots of people. Since I work here." She laughs. "What's her name?"

"Mary O'Malley."

"Hmmm. I've never heard of her."

Great. Thought she meant Mom. "I mean I'm staying with Katherine Sullivan." Get me out of here.

"Are you trying to mess with me, Liam?"

"Sorry." Did I blow it already? I'm confused.

"I'm just kidding. I know Kat. Her sculptures are famous."

"I haven't really seen much of her work."

Silence. Awkward. What should I say?

"So how do you like the cinnamon roll?" She smiles. Again.

"Amazing." Smile back.

Definitely amazing.

NOTICING THE SILENCE

Haven't heard a siren once since I got to Lakeshore.

No sirens when I'm walking around Main Street. Not down at the beach. It's especially quiet when I'm in Kat's studio. Doesn't anything bad ever happen here?

Sirens are a constant at home. Police. Fire. Ambulance. Each has a different sound. Police siren makes short *bip, bip, bips* with a quicker siren. Fire siren is deeper and drawn out. Ambulance siren isn't quick like the cops. Not slow like the big engines. Somewhere in the middle.

No sirens in two weeks. No black-and-whites driving around, either. No cops standing in stores. None walking the streets.

Nothing.

Nothing but the sound of my brain on repeat—thinking about that girl at the bakery.

Looking at titles on the shelves in the living room. Kat's in the dining room. Eating dessert with company. A carpenter. Emergency-room nurse. Owner of the movie theater. Petty officer in the coast guard. Ballet teacher at Kat's art academy. Organic farmer. She enjoys "good food with good friends." They're all okay. And it *was* good food.

The only awkward moment was when the ballet woman asked Kat how her new sculpture was coming along. Kat said she's been "a little blocked, preoccupied."

In Minneapolis I usually watch TV after dinner. Kat doesn't own one. She said she doesn't like anyone telling her how to think. Tyrell would think I was crazy if he knew that I hadn't watched TV since I got here.

Start after the books about Jean-Michel Basquiat. Georgia O'Keeffe. Wassily Kandinsky. I've seen something by each of them during field trips to the Minneapolis Institute of Arts. And Kiki Smith. She had an exhibit at the Walker. It was kind of creepy. A room that looked like a kitchen with a statue of a girl about Declan's size. The girl was staring up at the ceiling with spooky eyes. Gave me bad dreams. Definitely not my favorite exhibit.

Next shelf: Claes Oldenburg, Diego Rivera, Elizabeth Peyton, Andy Warhol, Carrie Mae Weems, Pablo Picasso.

Picasso? Home run. Cover has the painting from art class at Saint Al's.

Lift the heavy book off the shelf. Open to an amazing painting.

Pablo Picasso, *Guernica*, 1937. Oil on canvas, 138 by 306 inches. So that'd be twenty-five feet wide by twelve feet tall. About the size of my favorite phoenix graffiti piece in Minneapolis. This painting is the second most beautiful thing I've ever seen. Maybe third. If I count that girl at the bakery.

Guernica has only gray, black, and white paint. Scene of horror and chaos. People. Horse. Bull. Large lightbulb near the center of the painting. Beams of light illuminate different views of the horse's head.

Cubism. Very cool. Love to be able to do something like this.

In the painting an arm comes from nowhere holding a candle with one of those glass things around the flame. Woman cradles her dead baby. Screams up toward heaven. Probably wondering where God is. Man trampled by a frantic horse. Severed arm still hanging onto a broken sword. Person on the right looks like he's drowning. Eyes bugging out in panic.

Picasso wants me to know something horrible happened.
I got it.
Get out my blackbook. Work on some new sketches

while *Guernica's* fresh in my mind. Trying to draw some of the paintings I've seen in Kat's artist books. More traditional things instead of just *St. B* tags.

Want to come up with my own style. Want to step up to the plate.

Dying to paint a graffiti masterpiece. Like that incredible phoenix piece. Much more complicated than tags. Design something here in Lakeshore then spray paint it when I get back to Minneapolis in a couple of months. If I never move up to a three-color masterpiece, I'll only be a tagger. A scribbler.

Need to work hard. Come up with something that'll make people stop and stare.

Prove that I'm a graffiti writer. Maybe even an artist.

CRUISING THROUGH TOWN

Kat and I are headed back from an organic farm. We got chicken and beef from the farmer woman who was at dinner. Picked blueberries. Cucumbers. Very cool place. Rode along just for something to do. Weird to drive everywhere. Things are spread out. No city buses. No light-rail. In Minneapolis I walked everywhere.

We wait at the stoplight. Across from a park. Kids play pickup baseball on the fields.

"Look at that, Liam. America's game at its best."

"I guess."

"You guess? That's all you can say, Mr. Hotshot Short-stop?"

I smile. "Playing on my school team changed my opinion about baseball."

"Really? I thought you loved it."

"Not exactly."

"You don't have to tell me . . ."

"It's okay. I got recruited to play at a rich Catholic school in the suburbs."

"Your mom told me about that. She said it was a great opportunity for you."

"I don't know."

"A top-notch school."

"Some people think so." Not me.

"Sorry," she says. "Go ahead."

"First day of practice. The whole team had on perfect two-hundred-dollar Nike cleats. I stood there in my scuffed twenty-buck, bottom-of-the-clearance-box Adidas. They expected me to get the team cleats. Told me no Crusader would wear crap like my Adidas. I didn't have money to get cleats like they had." Talking way too much.

"So you quit after the first practice?"

"No. Later. I just stopped going."

"They continued to give you a hard time because of your *shoes*?"

"I was never like those guys. They all played together on elite teams since they were little kids. I played in city park leagues with my friends. I wasn't one of them."

"That's why you quit?"

"They didn't want a freshman to be playing varsity."

"So?"

"My teammates peed on my uniform in the locker room."

"They did *what*?"

"I opened my locker to get dressed for a game. My uniform was soaked in pee."

"Are you kidding me? What did the coach say?"

"I didn't tell him. It doesn't matter. I quit. Hey, the light changed."

"Wait a minute . . ."

"No big deal. Green light."

"Actually, it is a big deal, Liam. You should've gotten the coach involved."

HONK! HONK!

"Better move on, Kat."

PRETENDING LIKE SHE KNOWS

Kat doesn't know anything about me.

So I quit Saint Al's baseball. So I'm not wearing a Crusaders uniform. Who gives a crap? I hated Saint Al's and every jerk on that baseball team. She has no idea what it's like to want to fit in. To spend every day feeling like you're invisible. Or worse, like a loser.

Easier to quit than cry.

Better to be angry than sad.

She thinks that crap at Saint Al's was a big deal?

How about this, Kat? When your older brother tricks you into doing something dangerous. Tells you he has your back. Takes off when a rival banger shows up. Forgets about you. And you end up with the barrel of a silver Glock rammed against your head.

That's the definition of a big deal.

RESISTING BOREDOM

Walk up and down Main Street. Same things again, again. And again. I've grown bored of the scene outside my window. Nothing to draw. Nothing about to happen. Need some of the chaos of my hood.

Drowning in Lakeshore.

Walk up to the entrance of the hardware store. Mr. Philosopher working? He'd probably make me do his job. Again.

A couple stands next to a riding lawn mower. Shiny green paint. Padded yellow seat. Black steering wheel. Nicer than most cars in my hood. Sign taped to the windshield says this company's been creating beautiful lawns for more than twenty-five years.

We used to have a decent lawn. Even a backyard. Then Dad came home. Drunk. Got mad at Mom. He screamed, "You miserable bitch!" Hit Mom. Hit Kieran. Hit me. Set the couch on fire. Finally passed out. Mom snuck me, Kieran, Patrick, and Fiona away. She told us, "No more." Lived at a shelter for a while. Went home to get some things. Dad took everything but the dining-room table and chairs. He closed the bank accounts. Canceled the credit cards.

No one's seen him since.

HELPING KAT IN HER STUDIO

She's trying to get serious about her latest metal sculpture. I move things around to give her more space. Scrape hunks of dried clay off the floor. Used tubes of paint are supposed to go into the garbage. Grab them.

Hide the tubes in my pockets. Wait. Take them back out.

"You want me to throw all these away?" I say.

"Sure."

"There's still paint in some of them."

"Where?"

Hold the handful up. "I'll take these if you don't want them."

"Okay. But I've got plenty of new tubes that I'd be happy to share with you."

"These are fine." Into my pockets.

Kat walks over to the big closet against the wall. Opens the doors. Every shelf filled. Every supply a real artist would ever need. Colored pencils. Crayons. Markers. Erasers. One whole section of spray paint. She carries a couple of two-by-three-foot plastic bins over to the table. Filled with tubes of paint.

"This is my stash. See any other colors that you might need?"

"Sweet. How about all of them?"

She laughs. "Are you working on a new project? I thought that graffiti taggers—sorry—writers, used only Sharpie markers or spray paint."

"I'm thinking about trying some new things. Besides graffiti."

"Sounds interesting."

"I don't know. Maybe some painting."

"I'd be happy to look at your work if you ever want to show me."

Never shown anyone my sketches. Not Tyrell or Sean. Not even Patrick. "I can go get my blackbook if you want. The one you got me."

"Great. I'll clear a space here on the table."

I return and begin to show Kat a few pages. All the different sketches from around the JFKs.

"I love this one," she says. She points to my piece of the girl playing hoops back in the projects. "Such a colorful contrast between her traditional dress and the jersey."

Turn to my ideas for lettering. Sketches that copy Basquiat's work. Cubism.

Not my *St. B* tags. Flip through those pages as fast as I can. I stop on a sketch.

"This is from your bedroom window," Kat says. "It's beautiful."

Shrug. "It's okay."

"You're really very talented, Liam. Your work has great range."

Shrug.

"How serious are you about painting?"

"I spend most of my time just trying to improve my graffiti."

"I encourage you to give painting some thought, too. You might have a real talent for it."

Nod.

Really?

SWINGING ON THE PORCH

Back and forth in the hammock. Shaded by a huge oak tree. Peaceful. Lake Michigan waves roll in and out. Same thing again and again. Know what to expect.

What's that? Sounds like girls' voices from the sand-covered street. Singing a song.

I glance quickly. Spot three girls. Turn and look down at my fingernails. Can still see them out of the corner of my eye.

"Hey!" Someone's waving at me.

Wave back in a very uncool way. Helpless feeling. If Tyrell and Sean were here, we'd be punching each other. Acting like fools.

Heading my way. Stand up and look cool, O'Malley. Try.

"What's good?"

"How's it going?" says the beautiful one from the bakery.

"Okay." Be smooth. "Hey, Sara."

"Hi, Liam." She turns to her friends. "Hey, this is the new summer guy I told you about."

"You're right," says one of the other girls. "He does have gorgeous blue eyes."

"Thanks a lot, big mouth." Sara crosses her arms.

My face feels like a bad sunburn.

Then she smiles her smile. Sara, cool as Lake Michigan.

"Hey, Liam." One throws up a peace sign. "Where're you staying?"

"Right here." Point at Kat's.

"With the Lady Artist?"

Again? Everyone must call her that. "I guess that's Kat's nickname."

"That's what everyone calls her." Sara shrugs.

"Oh." Should I say something funny? How about something clever?

"Well . . . we better get going."

"Yeah. Me too." Very stupid. Where's Sean when I need to punch someone?

"See ya around, Liam." Sara waves.

"Okay." Extremely clever.

They walk away. Sara stops. "We swim at the public beach, right down there, every afternoon. We play beach volleyball. The locals and the summer kids just hang out. Come down sometime if you want."

"Okay." Sweet.

MISSING MY HOOD

Wish I were hanging out with Tyrell and Sean.

Park league baseball. Video games. Sneaking into Target Field. Watching the Twins. TV.

Wonder what's going on at O'Malley manor. Check in at home. Need to hear familiar voices. I miss Minneapolis.

"Hello."

"Hey, Declan."

"Liam!"

"How're things?"

"I got a dinosaur from Goodwill."

"Cool."

"A brachiosaurus."

"With the long neck?"

"Yeah. But he's not scary."

"Good."

"It's a nice kind," he says.

"Very cool."

"Yeah. Very cool."

"Where's Mom, Declan?"

"Next door getting something."

"Where?"

"What?"

"Whose apartment?"

"Murphys'."

Probably sneaking a smoke with Mrs. Murphy. She doesn't know I know.

"Then let me talk to Patrick, okay?"

"You hafta say the helping word first."

"Please."

"He's not here."

"Where is he?"

"I want to talk to Liam now," Fiona interrupts. Loud and close.

"No, Fiona. It's my turn. Um, Patrick's with Tommy because Kieran has to be in jail because he shot a gun up in the air and he has to go to the court then, and maybe he has to go to a bigger jail then because he did a bad thing, because of the gun, so Patrick's not here."

Declan takes a deep breath. Goes back to arguing with Fiona.

"Patrick's with Tommy?" I tense up. That Irish Mafia loser. "*Hello!* Is anyone there?"

"*Shhh,* be quiet or you going to get us into trouble, Liam." Fiona sighs. "We're not supposed to be using the phone."

"Give me back the phone," Declan interrupts. "I was talking to Liam first."

THUD.

"Saints preserve us." Mom says. She's back. "Can't I even go next door for a breath of fresh air without you two fighting? Why is the phone on the floor?"

"Mom?" C'mon.

"Who broke the phone? This is why we can't have anything nice. Happy?"

"Hello?"

"Both of you go to your rooms . . . NOW. Never a moment of peace."

Click.

"MOM!"

I push redial. Why is Patrick with Tommy?

Annoying busy signal. I hang up. Try redial again. Busy signal.

Patrick should not be hanging out with *anyone* from Irish Mafia. Especially not Tommy.

QUESTIONING THE MENU

Kat takes me to the fancy Asian restaurant on Main Street. Order? I know what white rice is. Not so sure about all of this other stuff.

"Have you decided?" Kat closes her menu.

"Ummm." I have no idea what any of this food is.

"The fried rice is wonderful."

Place our orders. I'm starving.

"So, you've been here about three weeks."

"Seventeen days."

Kat laughs. "Okay, seventeen days. How's it going so far?"

"Okay." Mean it, I guess.

"Sure?"

"Yeah." Not great. Not horrible.

"Have you met any other kids?"

"A few." Sara.

"Good. I ran into Hank Masterson at the hardware store. He's glad I have a decent young man staying with me for the summer."

Mr. Philosopher said I'm a decent young man?

"Hank was the first person I met when I moved here from NYC. He explained the lay of the land here in this little town. He's a good guy."

"Why did you move here again?"

"I needed a change of scenery."

"Oh."

"Actually, I just needed a change. Period."

"Why?"

"New York offered too many opportunities for me to mess up my life."

I nod.

Waiter delivers our food. "Green curry with tofu, extra spicy for the lady, and fried rice with chicken, mild for the gentleman. Enjoy."

"Lakeshore allows me to focus on my art and remember what's important to me."

"Right." This food is what's important to me. Smells so good.

"Enough of that. Let's dig in while it's still hot."

Best thing I've ever eaten. Need to slow down. Don't eat like a pig. Kat's using chopsticks. Don't want to look like an idiot. Stick with the fork.

"It's good to meet some kids your age. Plenty of locals, and the summer kids. Quite a few from Chicago have summer homes here."

"Nice."

"Well, you'll let me know if you need anything, or if there's something you want to do, right?"

"Okay."

"By the way, I'm going to ten o'clock Mass tomorrow morning. Would you like to join me?"

"Ummm." I actually get a choice? Don't really want to. "Sure."

HURRYING TO THE BAKERY

It's after Mass, which wasn't so bad. I like the ritual of it. It's always the same, so I know what to expect. The priest gave a decent homily. Kat and I left after communion. Nice surprise. Mom always makes us stay until the very end.

Going to meet Sara. Jog. Slow down. Try to get there without looking stupid. We're going to take her dog for a walk. No need to be in a hurry. Yes, there is.

Open the creaky screen door. Two men and a woman standing in the middle of the room.

"I wonder if it's those troublemakers who gather down by the ice-cream parlor." The man's wearing a *Lake Michigan (no salt added)* shirt.

Woman folds her arms. "Could be. I wonder why it's just showing up now."

Dog barks outside.

"All I know is graffiti's not good for business, what with the summer residents arriving," the other man says.

Don't want to be here. Where's Sara? Looking out the screen door. Big golden Labrador looks up at me. Sara waves.

"It's just plain ugly. Like a dog marking his territory." Woman scrunches her nose up.

What the . . . ? Why do people always hate street art? It's

just another art form. The same thing shows up in a frame at a museum and everyone loves it. Look at Keith Haring. Basquiat. When art collectors saw their stuff on the walls in NYC, they loved it so much they convinced Basquiat and Haring to start doing the same thing on canvases.

The three keep talking. "We should probably get the police involved before it becomes a bigger problem."

"Don't want the tourists to think we have riffraff in Lakeshore," man in the no-salt shirt says.

Try not to look guilty. Open the door.

"Hey, Liam." It's Sara. "This is Bowzer."

"Hey, fella." I rub his head. Wish I had a dog. He lifts his paw.

"That's his way of saying hello."

"Oh." Shake back.

The woman walks toward us. "Sara?"

"This is Liam, Mom."

"Liam?" She smiles. Same as Sara's.

"Yes, ma'am." Catholic-school manners.

"Do you have a last name, Liam?"

"O'Malley."

"I don't think I know your parents' names."

Silence.

Sara lays her hand on my shoulder. "He's staying in town for the summer."

"Nice to meet you, Liam. Welcome to Lakeshore."

I nod. "Thank you."

"And this is my dad." Sara points to the taller man. Polo shirt. Collar up.

"A summer resident." He stares at me.

Look him right in the eye. No hand out for a shake?

"Where are you staying, Liam?"

None of your business, boojie. "Minneapolis."

STROLLING BY THE HARBOR

"My parents are kind of nosy." Sara shrugs.

"That's okay." Very nosy.

"I love this harbor." She shades the sun from her eyes. "It's so peaceful."

"Looks like a lake." City lake in Minneapolis. Minus the people, tall buildings, and thumping tunes.

We walk. The path winds along the harbor. I hold Bowzer's leash.

"Tell me about your family, Liam."

"Not much to tell. Me, Mom, Kieran, Patrick, Fiona, Declan."

"Wow. Five kids?"

"Yeah."

"Dad?"

"Nope. Haven't seen him since I was seven."

"I'm sorry."

"I'm not."

We walk past row after row of docked boats. Bowzer barks at two ducks. Tighten my grip on the leash.

"So, what about your family?"

"Me, Bowzer." She bends down. Rubs his head. "Mom and Dad."

"No brothers or sisters?"

"Just me."

"Should I say sorry?"

"Yes. I always wanted brothers and sisters. My parents pay too much attention to me."

"So?"

"So they already have my whole life planned out for me. I'll graduate from Lakeshore High School with honors, get my undergraduate degree in pre-law from the University of Michigan, then go on to Harvard Law."

"That's bad?"

"Horrible," she says. "I want to be a Coastie."

Coastie? "Why not a lawyer?"

"Because I want to do something completely different."

Pause. Don't want to sound stupid but have to ask. "What's a Coastie?"

"I want to join the coast guard." She smiles.

"So tell them that's what you want." Right. Like it's that easy.

"I've tried. They won't talk about it."

"You're going to be a sophomore right?" Another thing we have in common.

"Yep."

"Then you've got lots of time to convince them."

"My parents don't look at it that way. They keep telling

me I only have three years to get my life in order. I need to be preparing now to get into U of M."

We stop. At a gate in front of white-and-red buildings. Big sign reads: *United States Coast Guard. Lakeshore Station.*

"This is my something completely different." She points.

"Very cool."

"What do you want to be, Liam?"

"I haven't really thought about it that much." Famous graffiti writer? "Maybe an artist."

APPROACHING THREE GUYS

They're standing in front of the pizza place. Wearing beaters. Baggie khakis. Red bandannas. Checking out *St. B* tagged on the bench. My handstyle looks impressive.

Are they Bloods? Definitely wearing colors.

Sara squints. "Did they tag that bench?"

"What do you mean?" Can't tell her it's mine. She sounds angry.

"Yo." One of them takes a step toward us.

I lift my chin. City way of acknowledging someone. "What's good?"

"You here for the summer, man?" one of them says. He's wearing a red Yankees cap. The bill's tilted to the left. Meaning he bangs.

"Yeah."

"You from Chicago?"

Chicago? "Minneapolis."

"You live in the city, cuz?"

What the . . . ? "Yeah."

"Decent. Know anything about *this*, man?" He throws up a lame version of the hand sign for Bloods.

Gang wannabes. "Yeah. Some." I try to keep from laughing out loud at these fools. "But I don't bang."

"Why, are you chicken shit?" They high-five each other.

Got no time for these poseurs. Walk away.

"See this, homeboy?" Guy with the Yankees hat points to my tag. "STB, baby. Submit to Bloods. Don't you forget it, man."

"Knock it off, guys." Sara rolls her eyes. "We don't live in the hood."

Want to tell her that I do. But maybe she won't want to hang out with me. Keep walking.

Then I stop. Turn around. "Hey!" I throw down the sign for Bloods. Showing disrespect.

They just stare. Stupid looks on their faces. "I thought so." I smirk and turn around. STB? Yeah, right.

I jog. Need to catch up to Sara.

WANTING MORE INFORMATION

Been awake since about four this morning. Can't stop thinking about everything. So many things in my head. Sara. Basquiat. Picasso. Sara.

After breakfast I take the back way to the library. Past the harbor. Huge sailboats tied to docks. Tall masts stand like skeletons. Some boats are anchored farther out in the water. Sara said people use small dinghies to get to shore. Living on a sailboat would be very cool.

I climb up the grassy hill to the library. Woman unlocks the front door.

"Good morning." She holds the door open. Her name tag says Librarian.

"Morning."

Help and reference desk. Best place to start my research. Three middle-aged men walk past, over to the computer stations along the wall.

"May I help you?" Librarian says.

"Do you have an art section?"

"Yes. Are you looking for something specific?"

"Well, anything about Pablo Picasso. And Jean-Michel Basquiat."

"Biographies or examples of their work?"

"Both?"

"Picasso, yes. Basquiat, maybe. Let's head over to the art section. I'll show you what we have."

Past the teen section. *The Chocolate War* propped on the top shelf. Never finished that at Saint Al's.

We get to the art section. She hands me two books. *Picasso: Art as Autobiography* and *Picasso and American Art.*

"This second book is great because it talks about Picasso's influence on contemporary American artists."

"Good."

"Now Basquiat. Here we are." She holds up *Basquiat: A Quick Killing in Art.*

"Thank you."

"Happy to help." She smiles. "Let me know if you need anything else."

Sit at the table closest to the window. That way I can look at the sailboats. Open the book about Basquiat.

Jean-Michel Basquiat said that his father was abusive.

Basquiat's teachers remembered him as uncommonly talented but very angry.

Basquiat ran away from home at fifteen.

Basquiat's work reflected his urban surroundings.

Nobody could ignore Jean-Michel Basquiat.

HEADING BACK TO THE HOUSE

In a hurry. Grocery bag filled with books about Basquiat, Picasso, NYC graffiti artists. Got *The Chocolate War,* too. Pass a small house completely covered by huge rosebushes. Elderly man with a long silver pole in one hand. Cane in the other. It's Mr. Philosopher. Looks right at me.

"Give me a hand, will ya?"

Not again. "Sure."

"Liam, right?"

"Yeah. Clarence?"

"Most folks call me Hank."

"Right."

"I'm trying to trim these rosebushes, but I can't reach up high enough." He drops the long pole. Picks up something that looks like huge scissors. "Take these clippers and give it a try." Hands them to me. "You're a lot taller than I am."

Great. Never done this before. Put my bag of books down.

"Now, look above you. See that tangled branch?"

"I think so." What if I screw up?

"Use the lower end of the clippers and cut straight through."

Careful to only get one branch. "Here?" I say.

"That's it. Cut it clean now."

Wood's thick. Not easy to cut.

"I'm going to have to really crank on this, Hank."

"Go ahead. Just take your time."

"Okay." Do this right. Push hard. *CRRRAAACK.* Branch lands next to my feet. "How's that?"

"Good job." He picks up the fallen branch. "Thanks."

"You're welcome."

He cuts a few red roses off. "Smell that beauty." Holds one out toward me.

"Okay." Reminds me of my third-grade teacher who always smelled like this. She hung my drawings on the class bulletin board. "Yeah, it's nice." Petals look like red velvet. A miniature painting.

"My wife—God rest her soul—loved roses. All kinds. But this one here, this was her favorite."

Nod. Hank was married.

"The things just keep growing, so I've gotta keep them trimmed. When these things get too wild, you can't see their beauty anymore."

I nod. He keeps talking.

"We planted this one the day after we moved into this house. Forty-two years ago."

"Really?" Forty-two years in *Lakeshore*?

"Yessir. Moved up here from Detroit. Couldn't take the crime in the city anymore."

"Oh." Don't know what else to say. "I've got to get going, Hank."

"What's your hurry? Sit down and take a load off. You want some lemonade?"

"I've got to get back to Kat's."

"Okay, then. Thanks for your help."

"No big deal." Start walking.

"Wait." He lifts my bag. "You forgot your groceries."

SPENDING TIME WITH SARA

Hanging out. In her backyard. Goofing around with Bowzer. He walks over to a huge maple tree. Lies in the shade.

"It's muggy out here. You want to watch TV?" Sara says.

"Sure." Thank you, God. "I haven't watched TV in almost a month. Kat doesn't have one."

"Come on, it's in the family room." She walks in the back door.

"You heard the woman. Let's go, Bowzer."

A room that's almost as big as our whole apartment in Minneapolis. Big-screen TV on one side. Pool table on the other.

"Nice place."

"My dad likes his toys. He likes to unwind after a long day in the OR."

"OR?"

"Operating room. He's a surgeon," she says.

"Hmmm." She's rich. Doesn't act like it, though.

"You want to play pool instead?"

"Okay. But I have to warn you, I'm pretty good." Tyrell, Sean, and I use the table covered with wads of gum and spilled pop at the community building. Should probably take it easy on her. Be a gentleman. No reason to make her feel bad. Even if her dad's a polo-wearing boojie.

Sara wins every game.

"You shouldn't have tried to let me win." She pokes my arm.

"I didn't." I *was* trying.

"Yes."

"Well, only in the beginning."

"A gentleman, right?"

I laugh. "Yeah, or something like that."

"Let's watch TV." She tosses me the remote.

"If you insist."

APPROACHING THE STOP SIGN

Thick black letters cover the letters S-T-O-P. Can't stop St. B.

Did another tag a few days ago. Hope everyone notices I changed up my handstyle. Again. Bubble design. This one looks like it's made of balloons that were blown up and tied at the bottom. My favorite. So far.

Group of people gathered nearby. They don't look happy. Staring at my work. Have to pass them to get back to Kat's house. Keep walking. Try to look like I belong here.

"STB? What's STB?" Man wearing plaid trousers.

The signature of a graffiti writer can't be ignored. Still. I look down at the sidewalk to ignore them.

"It's spray paint. Looks like graffiti."

"What does it mean? What's STB?"

Why does everyone think its STB?

"I've seen this kind of vandalism on CNN. Looks like gang stuff to me."

Gang stuff? I look up. Can't help it.

"Gangs?" Woman slaps her hands against her face. "In Lakeshore? I'm going to call town hall and find out what's going on."

Not again. It's only a tag.

"This garbage is an eyesore."

It's street art.

"This kind of stuff will scare the tourists away. The police need to take care of this."

I go around them. Can feel their eyes bearing down on me.

Someone whispers, "Do you know him?"

"No, but summer people *are* arriving."

"I think he's staying with the Lady Artist."

Shite.

OBSERVING MY SURROUNDINGS

Headed up and down Main Street with the rest of the summer people.

Think about Basquiat. The way he wrote things on walls in Brooklyn. Painted what he saw. Responded to his life. Made people know what was on his mind. Street artist. Tagged as SAMO©. For *same ol' shit*.

Created statements that forced people to think. Was a master of conceptual graffiti, which means the words he wrote were more important than what his tags looked like. Basquiat sprayed:

- Jimmy best on his back to the suckerpunch of his childhood files.
- We have decided the bullet must have been going very fast.
- A lot of bowery bums used to be executives.
- Plush safe he think.

Very cool. I could do something like Basquiat.

What have I seen in Lakeshore? White sun. White clouds. White skin. White clothes. White beach toys. White fudge. White buildings. SAMO©. SAMO©. SAMO©.

Wait.

White buildings mean white walls. Fresh canvases for a street artist. Like Basquiat. A way to tell people what's on my mind. Right, Jean-Michel? I feel that adrenaline thing. Run. Back to Kat's as fast as I can. Need my blackbook. Want to force these people to think.

I'll give them something more involved than a tag. More artistic. Make them see what I'm trying to say.

VISUALIZING MY VOICE

On the pages of my blackbook. Working on something important. Much more involved than St. B or the Irish Mafia shamrock. Experimenting with ideas for a masterpiece. Has to be big. And Kat's book about Basquiat said that it has to have at least three colors for the design to be considered a piece. Sizes. Letter styles. Practice until they're exactly right. Clear. Purposeful. Intentional.

Time to move up to something more complicated. Don't want to stay a tagger my whole life. Can't do anything like that amazing phoenix piece. Not yet. But I could probably do a conceptual graffiti piece like Basquiat. He used words to show where he came from. I'll create a piece to make a statement about me. About my life. Colorful conceptual graffiti.

Everyone will see what I have to say.

They'll know where I'm coming from.

JOGGING OVER TO HANK'S

Going to help him paint his garage.

See a kid and his dad playing baseball at the playground.

Got a couple of minutes to watch this.

They're just throwing the ball back and forth. The dad gives pointers to his son. Laughing. Having a good time. How nice.

Yeah, right.

Who gives a crap? Basquiat never played catch with his dad, either.

WRAPPING A T-SHIRT AROUND EACH SPRAY CAN

So they don't clang together in my backpack. Dying to spray my first masterpiece. Wanted to do this two nights ago, but I was too tired from painting at Hank's. Fully rested now. Tonight's the night.

Pull on my black hoodie. Need to blend in with the dark. Walk barefoot through the living room. Don't wake Kat up. Clock on the mantel bongs twelve.

Quietly close the door.

Showtime.

SCREAMING WHAT LAKESHORE NEEDS TO SEE

Find a spot on the large wall of the bathhouse. It's the entrance to the public beach. Biggest empty space I could find. Light from the front of the building is just bright enough to see what I'm doing.

Bandanna around my mouth and nose. Hood over my head. Look all around. Can of Midnight Black out of my backpack. Whole outline will be black. Remember to spray like the can is an extension of my hand.

CLIKCLAKCLIKCLAKCLIKCLAK. Plastic cap off. Remember to stay close to the wall. Move quick for a clean outline. Just like Basquiat. Look again. Now. Press down on the nozzle.

PSSSSSSSSSSSSSSSSSSSSSSSSST. Love this sound.

So far so good. Hardly any drips. See headlights. Hide. Crawl to other side of the bathhouse. Waiting for the dark to return, so I can get the outline done soon. Brightness turns the corner. Disappears.

Need to have time to fill in the letters with a second color. Relax. Work quickly but carefully. This needs to be perfect. Don't screw it up by going too fast.

Done. Midnight Black in. Shock Blue out. Fill color.

CLIKCLAKCLIKCLAKCLIKCLAK. Start again.

PSSSSSSSSSSSSSSSSSSSSSSSSSSST. Very cool. Even better than the sketch in my blackbook. Shock Blue is perfect. Great color. Careful not to let the paint drip down onto the outline.

Bright flash. Headlights again? Another car. Drop to the ground. What the . . . ? The car stops. Heart's racing. Door opens. Spotlight. Lie still. Footsteps. Don't move.

Not one muscle.

Walking this way? Don't even breathe.

"Base? This is one-five-two. Over."

A cop? Crap.

"I'm at the site." Beam from her spotlight swings all over. "It's empty. Nothing going on."

She didn't see me? Didn't see my piece? Spotlight must've shined everywhere but on my piece.

"Roger that."

Car door slams. Cop drives away.

Wait. Don't be stupid. Stay still. Everything's quiet. Ha. Luck of the Irish. Looking around. Hang on.

Now. Get this piece done. Get out of here.

Finishing the Shock Blue fill.

Only the glow left. Blue in. Tornado Red out.

CLIKCLAKCLIKCLAKCLIKCLAK. Start at the top left-hand corner of the piece.

PSSSSSSSSSSSSSSSSSSSSSSSSSSST. Follow the letters all the

way back around to the starting point. Red because it demands attention.

Done.

Step back to take another look.

STREET ART: LIVE FROM THE HOOD

Just like in my blackbook. Amazing. More like something Basquiat would've done. Artistic lettering style. Beautiful.

Feel like I just turned a double play. Complete satisfaction.

Ha. More than a whisper of graffiti in Lakeshore now. Supplies into my backpack. Hands covered in paint. Three colors this time.

WHOOP, WHOOP. What the . . . ? Siren?

"Lakeshore Police! Stop where you are!"

Hell, no! Grab my backpack. Run. Down Main Street. Alley behind Sara's bakery. Hide somewhere back there. Cop car right behind me. Spotlight following every step. Get off the street. Not behind the bakery. Cop can drive back there. Heading back toward Kat's.

No.

The school. Get to the woods behind the school. Where's the alley near the school? Spotlight from the squad car shines on the street to my left. I race through the alley.

Heart pounding. Cut across to the street on the other side of these houses.

Remember ding-dong-ditching with Kieran when we were little kids. What would he do now? No way to outrun the cop. Where should I go? Hide. Find someplace. Now.

Open garage. Perfect. Hide between the car and the wall. Hoodie off. Cop saw me. Shove it in my backpack. With my bandanna and spray cans. Best to hide everything here. Get it later. When it's safe.

Where's the cop?

Haven't seen her headlights. No spotlight. Don't be stupid. Stay in the garage. Wait. Completely silent. Breathe. Stay here as long as I have to. Until I'm sure she's not around anymore. Wait until daylight. It's got to be close to four o'clock by now. I can sit still for a couple of hours. Then jog back to Kat's. Make it look like I'm just out for a run.

Silence. Even my heart is slowing down. I did it. Maybe I actually finished my first piece *and* got away.

Wait.

Can't wait. Maybe take a quick look outside the garage. See what's what. Extremely quiet. Just one step . . .

"Freeze!" Bright light blinds me. "Lakeshore Police."

Crap. Now what? She's walking closer. Get rid of the spray cans. Evidence is in my backpack. Stash them someplace right now or I'm busted. Reach in to get the cans out.

"PUT YOUR HANDS UP!" Black handgun pointed at me. Glock.

Freeze.

"SHOW ME YOUR HANDS!"

Arms up. Hands out.

"Get on the ground. Now."

Dropping to my knees. Glock two feet away from me.

My face on the pavement.

"Put your hands behind you." Her knee grinds my body onto the concrete. She slaps the handcuffs around my wrists. "Gotcha, you little punk."

FIGHTING TO STAY CALM

In the back of a police car, my body's twisted sideways. No room for my legs. Arms pinned behind my back. Every muscle tight. Have to pee. In so much trouble. Can't believe I'm sitting in the back of a squad car. In handcuffs.

"What's your name?"

"Liam."

"And?"

Silence.

"We can make this easy or difficult, Liam."

"O'Malley."

"Do you have any ID?"

"School?"

"That's fine."

"It's in my backpack."

She reaches over and grabs my stuff off the seat.

"I'll get it for you." I lean forward.

"Can you take these handcuffs off?"

She looks at me in the rearview mirror. "I've got it." Opens the big compartment of my backpack.

Cans of spray paint are in there. "No, wait!"

She turns around. "Are you refusing to cooperate?" Stares at me through the plexiglass.

Calm down. "No. My ID's not in that part. It's in the small pocket on the front.

She opens my wallet. "Where's Saint Aloysius Gonzaga High School?"

"Minneapolis."

"Oh, city kid, huh?"

PACING IN A SMALL ROOM

Cop called it the closet.

Concrete walls. No windows. Bench drilled into the cement floor. Metal door with a peephole. Locked in a closet.

"I'm not a criminal." I don't belong here.

Back in the squad car, she asked me why I painted the graffiti. Wouldn't admit to doing it. Then about the STB tags. Told her I didn't know anything about them. Not a lie because I didn't do any STB tags. I did St. B tags. Then she brought me here.

Jail.

Kieran's in jail. He's been in juvenile detention plenty of times. I'm not Kieran.

Sit down. What's happening?

Cannot sit on this bench. Can't be still and wait. Cop said she'd be back. Need to walk. Don't even know what time it is. What time is she going to be back? Have to tell Mom. No place to walk when you're in jail. Not much room to move around in a closet. Mom's going to be furious. No. Worse than that. Disappointed. Again. And Kat? Maybe she won't have to know.

"Who's going to have to know about this?" I say to no one.

Silence.

Cannot believe this is happening. All I wanted to do was paint a piece like Basquiat. Prove I'm a graffiti writer.

Door opens.

"Let's go, Liam." Cop's carrying my backpack. And a small black case.

Follow her to a bigger room. Table. Two chairs. No windows.

"Have a seat." She takes a camera out of the small case. "Put your hands flat on the table. Palms down."

Click. Flash goes off. Picture of my hands. Splattered. Midnight Black. Shock Blue. Tornado Red.

"Flip them over so your palms are up."

Click. Flash. Evidence.

"I need to inventory the contents of your backpack."

I'm done.

She takes out three cans of spray paint. Black from Hank's hardware store. Blue and red from Kat's studio. Next comes my hoodie. Bandanna.

"What's this?" She lifts my blackbook.

Shite.

She opens the cover.

"That's mine!"

"Calm down."

"It's private."

"It's evidence in a crime."

"A crime?" Play stupid.

"Exactly." She quickly looks through everything. Page after page filled with sketches of my ideas. She lands on a page. Crap. There's my final sketch for my *Street Art: Live from the Hood* piece.

Exactly like what's on the wall of the bathhouse.

Feel sick. Like I'm sitting here naked.

"Liam O'Malley, you are being charged with the misdemeanor crime of criminal damage to property under the graffiti ordinance law of MacDonald County. And with one count of misdemeanor fleeing while committing a crime."

Can't breathe.

"You have the right to remain silent. Anything you say can and will be used against you in a court of law. You have the right to an attorney present during questioning. If you cannot afford an attorney, one will be appointed for you. Do you understand these rights?"

Nod.

"Do you understand your rights, Liam?"

"Yes." My chin starts shaking. No crying.

"You have the right to call a parent or adult guardian. Who would you like to call?"

No one.

"Liam?"

"My mom's in Minneapolis."

"What's her number?"

"I'm staying with someone here."

"Name and number?"

Stare at the floor.

"I'm going to need to release you to an adult. You're a juvenile, so you can't stay in this jail. Otherwise I'll have to take you to a county foster home."

"Katherine Sullivan." The Lady Artist.

TRUDGING BACK BY THE SCENE OF MY CRIME

It's the day after I had a second Glock pointed at me.

It's five hours after Kat signed me out at the police station.

She told me I needed to go to the coast guard station with her. Dropped something off for that Coastie friend from dinner. Now Kat and I are on our way back.

No talking. A lot being said.

The closer we get to the beach, the harder it is to walk. Strong wind's blowing the sand all over. Stinging my face. Pull my hood down over my eyes. Grateful I don't have to look at Kat.

Big red sign at the public beach. "Warning: Extreme Danger! Swim at your own risk." The bathhouse is straight ahead.

She stops. "So there it is."

STREET ART: LIVE FROM THE HOOD

It covers the whole wall. Even more amazing in daylight. I'm proud of my work.

Still.

"Well, if you're going to make a statement, it might as well be big."

Huge gust of wind slams into us.

I don't know what to say.

She looks out at the pounding water of Lake Michigan. "Angry waves," she says.

Appropriate.

"There are so many artistic options for expressing yourself, Liam." She turns and walks away from my piece. "You chose one of the most troubling."

"Wait." I jog over to her. "What do you mean?"

"What do I mean? You got arrested."

"But I didn't hurt anybody." Look out into huge waves. "I was just trying to . . ."

"Liam. I'm not your mom. I'm not your boss. I consider you a fellow artist and I'm going to treat you that way."

I nod.

"But," she says, looking out toward the lighthouse, "I'm going to call you on it when I see you making less-than-wise choices."

"Okay. I just wanted to make something amazing."

"I get that, Liam, I do. But . . ."

"And you said graffiti is an art form. I just wanted to create something beautiful that people in Lakeshore don't usually get to see."

"And it *is* beautiful." She leans around me. Looks at my piece. "Your color choices are wonderful and the lettering style is very unique."

"Thanks. It's called wildstyle."

"But the way you created it was illegal and trespassing."

Gusts of wind almost knock us over.

"I created it so people around here would think differently about graffiti."

And so I could feel differently about Lakeshore. Maybe feel like I belong here.

BREAKING THE NEWS TO MOM

"YOU WHAT, LIAM?"

"I got arrested."

"What don't you get?"

"I don't know."

"What am I supposed to do with you?"

"Send me away?"

Click.

ARGUING ALL DAY

First with Kat. Then with Mom. Now with Sara.

"It was only a piece." Shake my head. "Actually, it was a legendary piece." I rep my work.

"It's graffiti, Liam."

"So?"

"So I live here." She crosses her arms.

I shove my hands in my pockets. "And?"

"We have summer people and tourists who come to Lakeshore to get away from what they see in the city. The money they spend in our little town for three months pays most of the business owners' bills for the whole year."

"I don't understand how my piece is something people would want to get away from."

"It's *graffiti*. People associate it with gangs and crime. If they see the same stuff here that they have to deal with at home, they'll find someplace new to spend the summer."

"Who cares? I'm just trying to do my thing. I wish I could spend my summer someplace else, too."

"That's nice. Maybe you should think of someone other than yourself."

"You know *nothing* about me, Sara." My stomach lurches. "So don't lecture me."

"Someone needs to."

"I'm out of here. I don't have to listen to your crap."

"Then don't, Liam."

I walk away, then turn around. "And you know what? I *do* live in the hood. And I *do* know about gangs. And I do know what it feels like to have a gun jabbed against the side of my head. But I'd still rather be back in my dangerous-as-hell hood than stuck here in Perfectville. Where nothing is ever allowed to happen."

TRYING TO GET AWAY FROM MYSELF

I need Lake Michigan.

Sprint toward the angry waves. Wind takes my breath away. No stopping. Sprinting across the beach. Into the fury. Can hardly hear myself think.

What did I do?

Arrested.

Complete idiot.

Running. Reach the shore. Feet crash into the water. Huge gust of wind slams me back. Stops me from going into the water. Preventing me from doing what I want. Shoves me away. Just like Mom, the headmaster at Saint Al's, the baseball team, everyone.

"GO TO HELL! ALL OF YOU CAN GO TO HELL!" I yell into the screaming wind. Out toward Minnesota.

I'm a wreck.

I bend low into the shortstop-ready position and charge into the pounding water. Waves punch my chest. Tackle me back toward shore. Knee-deep. Struggle to stay on my feet. Waiting for the next wave. Push forward as fast and as far as I can. Will not let this water beat me. Next one knocks me flat on my back. Wave rolls away. Kieran went away. Left me tagging for Irish Mafia. Right over Los Crooks.

"YOU SAID YOU HAD MY BACK, YOU DOUCHEBAG!"

Kieran wrecks everything.

Can't close my mouth. Wall of water crashes down onto me. Underwater. Tumbling. Spinning. Pummeled by the pounding surf. Struggling. Knocked over again and again. Just like Dad. The drunk who hit Mom, Kieran, me. Fractured our family. No phone calls. No playing catch in the yard. Not one single thing in seven years.

"I HATE YOU, YOU BASTARD!"

Dad wrecked it all.

Another wall of water. Dive straight into it. Force drags me along the sand on the bottom of the lake. Pins me down. Can't get up. Undertow takes me back out toward the deeper water. Can't control my body. Please help me, God. Can't move my legs to stand. Can't move my arms to swim. Can't do anything to help myself. Can't hold my breath. Get off the bottom. Help me, Saint Brendan. Panicking. Need to breathe. Get out of here. Help me. Someone please help me. Don't leave me here. Saint Brendan, pray for me. I don't want to die. Undertow's keeping me down. Can't fight anymore. Drowning. Drowning. Drowning.

No.

Won't let go. What can I do? Move. Try. Swim. Up to the

surface. Breathe. Breathe. Stay above the water. Open my eyes. Where am I? Find something.

Lighthouse.

The lighthouse. Straight out from Kat's. Tower in the sky. Beach to the left. Get to solid ground. Swim. Move. Thrown backward. Up and under the water. Out of control. Slam against something solid. The shore. Pull myself up onto the sand. I vomit. And vomit. Try to catch my breath. Lungs burn. Chest hurts. Ears ache. Whole body's been pounded. Close my eyes.

I'm battered.

I'm alive.

REMEMBERING SAINT BRENDAN'S PRAYER

Been saying these words since I was in second grade.

Shall I pour out my heart to You, confessing my manifold sins and begging forgiveness, tears streaming down my cheeks? Shall I leave the prints of my knees on the sandy beach, a record of my final prayer in my native land? Shall I then suffer every kind of wound that the sea can inflict? Shall I take my tiny boat across the wide sparkling ocean? O King of the Glorious Heaven, shall I go of my own choice upon the sea? O Christ, will You help me on the wild waves?

His words always made me feel safe when I was scared.
Now I understand what they mean.

Cross myself.

Grateful.

APPRECIATING A NEW NOTE ON THE FRIDGE

I notice it this morning.

"I am for an art that embroils itself with the everyday crap & still comes out on top." (Claes Oldenburg)

Definitely get this one.

Remember when I was Declan's age. Colored all the time. Dad hated it. Mom got me a box of sixty-four Crayola crayons for my birthday. Loved all those colors. Memorized every single name. Still angry that Dad broke all my crayons. He screamed and threw all the pieces into the garbage can.

I ran. Hid under my bed.

Waited until I was positive he was asleep that night. Snuck out. Dug through the garbage. Remember the crappy smell. Didn't matter. I picked every single broken piece of every single crayon out of the can. Cleaned each one. Taped all the pieces back together. Didn't work. No matter how careful I was.

Didn't cry. Used the pieces anyway.

ENJOYING THE FOURTH OF JULY PARADE

Sitting on the curb of Main Street.

Not as big as the parades in Minneapolis. It's okay. Little kids on decorated bikes. Lakeshore High School marching band. Mayor waves from a Chamber of Commerce float. Four Little League teams walk by in their uniforms. Dogs are dressed in red, white, and blue. Shirts and hats for dogs? Fire engine. Ambulance. Police car's being driven by the cop who arrested me. Look down at my fingernails until she's out of sight. Sirens blare on and off. Clowns run around, throwing candy. Always been afraid of clowns. Don't really know why.

Flatbed truck rolls up. Music's thumping. Sailors' Volleyball State Championship Runners-Up are passing. Truck's decorated with blue and gold balloons. Sara stands on the back. She looks at me.

I feel like a loser after our scene the other day. Mouth "Sorry." Give a pathetic wave.

She nods. "Me, too."

I smile.

"The beach this afternoon?" She shouts over the racket.

"Okay." My voice a little louder than my pounding heart.

"See you later."

"She's a nice girl." Kat smiles.

"Who?" Does she know?

"Sara? You could invite her over for dinner sometime."

Shrug.

"Oh, puhleeze."

"Fine. I'll ask her."

"Good."

Nice to just sit here. Observe everyone going past me. People all around me. Last time I went to a parade at home, the Bloods and Los Crooks started fighting. *BANGBANG-BANG.* Mass chaos. Tyrell and I fell facedown on the ground. Arms over our heads. Didn't want anyone to think we saw something. Never said a thing. Snitching makes you a punk in my hood.

Now everyone on both sides of the street is standing up. Guys taking their hats off. Everyone's clapping. Convertibles driving our way. Men riding in the cars. Waving to everyone.

War veterans.

Three Iraq vets in the first car. Don't look much older than I am. Soldier riding shotgun only has one arm. Vietnam vets roll up wearing old, faded camouflage shirts. Black-and-white POW/MIA flag's attached to the back bumper. Next the World War II soldiers. Elderly. Sitting safely on the seat.

I spot Hank. Hard to imagine him fighting in a war. He looks right at me. Salutes.

I do the same.

Soldier on.

DECIPHERING THE DECISION

Got my notification letter in the mail today.

According to the County District Attorney, I'm officially charged with a misdemeanor. I've been tagged as a criminal. If the cost to remove my piece had been over one thousand dollars, it would've been a felony. My *St. B* tags on the bench, garbage can, and stop sign definitely would've put me over. Didn't admit that to them.

Feel like I swallowed a golf ball.

Have to appear in court to plead guilty or not guilty. It says another letter with the date and time will be forthcoming.

Great. Something to really look forward to.

DREAMING ABOUT BASEBALL

Back at the championship game last summer. Minneapolis City Park League. Me. Tyrell. Sean. Saint Al's coach there to scout me. Went five for six. Home run. Offered a full-ride scholarship.

"Remember that arts camp we talked about?" Kat's voice wakes me up.

Where is she? Try to remember where I am. "What?" Must've fallen asleep on the couch.

"Lake Michigan Academy of Fine Arts. The place where I teach."

"Oh." Exhausted. Cut rosebushes for Hank all morning.

She walks into the living room. "The high-school visual arts section starts on July seventeenth. That's in two weeks. There may still be openings if you're interested."

"Openings?"

"For campers. Visual artists like you."

Never thought of myself as a visual artist. I'm a graffiti writer who ended up in jail. Me a visual artist? At an arts camp? I don't think so. "What does it cost? I don't have very much money."

"Nothing. You're living with me this summer, and I'm a faculty member."

"I still haven't found out when I have to go to court."

"The county attorney said you'd hear something by the end of the week. Remember?"

"I'll think about it."

"Fine." She walks out of the room. Back in. "You know your ship can't come in if you don't ever send it out in the first place."

What the . . . ?

She walks out the screen door. Lets it slam behind her.

SHIPPING IN OR OUT

Kat told me my ship can't come in if I don't send it out.

How does she know what my ship is?

Do I even know?

I've been thinking a lot about what it means to be an artist. I'd even told Kieran that I wanted to be one before I did that stupid shamrock tag. If I want to prove it, then maybe I should go to that camp for artists. Couldn't hurt.

But what happens if I figure out what my ship is, I send it out, and it still doesn't come in? What if I don't have what it takes to be a visual artist? What if Kat's only suggesting it because she wants to get me away from graffiti? Or, worse, that I'm her charity case.

Why does this have to be so confusing?

PULLING PICASSO OFF
THE SHELF

Open the book. Back to my favorite painting. *Guernica.* Horrible. Beautiful. Study what Picasso did. Considered his greatest masterpiece. Picasso painted a piece. What he saw going on around him. Picasso's very cool mural would fit right in on a wall in my hood.

Could I ever do something like this? Not really my style. What is?

Says here that "Picasso's painting style changed over the period of his life more than any other great artist. He was always trying new and different things." Always changing things up in his work. Picasso did his thing.

I want to learn how to do mine. Be brave enough to try different things. Don't want to just keep doing the same thing. Even Basquiat moved from wall to canvas. Went from tagging to painting.

At Lake Michigan Academy of Fine Arts maybe I can learn how to paint like Picasso. Maybe get good enough to paint a mural. Something huge like that amazing piece in the alley at home. Learn how to do it right. Create a mural using both spray and brushes? Don't know.

Maybe.

RAISING MY HAND IN THE WITNESS BOX

I'm standing next to the judge.

"Do you solemnly swear to tell the truth, the whole truth, and nothing but the truth, so help you God?" the county attorney says.

"I do."

"You may be seated. Please state your full name for the record."

"Liam Brendan O'Malley."

He reads all the details of my crime out loud. I say yes to every question he asks.

The judge turns toward me. "Do you understand the severity of your actions?"

"Yes." And no.

"Are you willing to make restitution for your crime?" He stares.

"Yes."

"Then I sentence you to repair and repaint the wall you've vandalized, complete thirty hours of community service by picking up garbage on Main Street and on the public beach, and serve probation for a period of one year. Probation will begin immediately in Lakeshore and continue in Minneapolis when you return at the end of the summer. I will forward a copy of your sentence parameters to the Juvenile Justice Center in Minneapolis."

Nod.

"If you do not complete your responsibilities, or break the rules of your probation, I will see to it that you spend time in a juvenile detention facility. Do you understand me, young man?"

"Yes, sir."

STRUGGLING WITH MY DECISION

"There are still openings at the camp," Kat reminds me. "I checked with the director."

"Oh." But I might look like a fool in front of everybody. Would have to be away from Sara every day for two weeks. What happens if I'm not as good as the others? What if I don't fit in? Not sure I want to take a chance. Gave up on baseball. Something I loved because I felt like a loser. Got to start making some changes. I don't know what to do.

Maybe I'm just . . .

"You don't have to let me know today. Soon, though."

Basquiat said that all he wanted was to be famous. He could learn to draw later.

I don't want to wait until later. I want to learn everything now, while I'm in Lakeshore. Don't know what's going to happen when I get back to Minneapolis, but I know I won't be able to go to an arts camp for free.

CLEANING UP MY MESS

Walk to the hardware store. Need to buy supplies. Have to spend most of the summer money Mom gave me. Ordered to clean up my art. Hope Hank's not here.

Brass bell clangs when I walk in. Hank's not at the front counter. Just the woman who works part-time. I walk down the narrow aisle in the middle. Toward the paint supplies. Past the shelves of spray paint.

Stop.

New colors. Mediterranean Teal. Sunburst Yellow. Meadow Green. Harbor Blue. Sunrise Red. These would look unbelievable on a huge piece. Sail Blue. Grass Green. Hot Red. Chrome Silver. I could create a very cool piece with—

"Need a hand with something?" a man's voice says.

Jerk around.

CRRAAAASH. Three cans hit the wood floor.

"No, thanks," I say.

It's Hank. He picks up the can of Harbor Blue. "I thought that was you, Liam."

Great. "Yeah." I put the others back up on the shelf.

"Got something that needs painting?"

"No. Um. I've got some other painting supplies to buy."

"What's on your list?"

"I'm good." I nod toward him. "But thanks, Hank."

"Let an old man earn his keep, will ya?"

Hope he doesn't ask too many questions. "Okay. I need extra-strength paint remover. A wire brush. A bucket for water."

"Surface?"

"What?"

"Where are you trying to remove paint from?"

"Concrete. A wall." Don't want to lie to him. "One of the walls on the bathhouse at the public beach. I. Umm. I painted a graffiti piece there."

"Graffiti, huh?"

We walk to the back of the store.

"Let's see . . . paint remover." He bends down to the lowest shelf. "Graffiti's illegal, isn't it?"

"Yeah." Wish it weren't.

"You don't strike me as a criminal, Liam."

Shrug. "I'm not."

He gets the rest of the supplies.

"Takes a man to admit his mistakes."

Nod.

Walk to the checkout counter.

"That should do you, then." Hank shakes my hand. "Don't be a stranger."

"Not in this town."

Hank gets it. Smiles.

Walk two blocks to the public beach. Sunny day. People everywhere. Open my backpack. Take out the vest I'm required to wear. Neon orange with reflective yellow strips. Criminal.

Stare at my masterpiece. Hope everyone will remember. Even after it's gone.

I cover *Street Art: Live from the Hood* with paint remover.

Back to an empty white wall.

Back to boring little Lakeshore.

SPENDING TIME WITH THE LOCALS

Been hanging out with Sara's Lakeshore friends when I'm not helping Kat or Hank. A few Chicago guys. Beach volleyball most afternoons. Pickup baseball games at the park.

Now Sara and I are at a beach party. Sitting around a bonfire. Orange glow of the flames looks cool against the dark sky.

Two guys walk up carrying a big red cooler. "Refreshments?" Everyone takes a beer.

Sara stands up. "You want one?"

A beer? "Umm . . ."

"Take a few, man. That graffiti mural you made was more than cool," one of them says.

"Thanks." I knew I wasn't the only one who thought so. I want to nudge Sara, but I don't.

"You're covered." Another guy gives me the okay sign. "No one's going to snitch."

Now what am I supposed to do?

"Take a hard lemonade if you want, dude." The bottle's in front of my face. Dad's voice screams in my head, "Take a drink, ya little girl!" Kieran and I promised each other. Kieran didn't care.

I take the bottle. Wait. "Actually, no. I'm on probation." Hand it back. "I'm good."

Sara sits back down. "Yeah, me too."

"It's cool if you want a beer," I say. Does she drink? "I can't because of the court thing."

"That's right." She leans close. "Juvenile delinquent." Smiles. "I don't really like the taste anyway."

"Oh."

She holds my hand. I like Sara. A lot. Want to tell her about the arts camp.

"How about some weed or something from the family medicine cabinet?" someone says. Don't know who. I definitely should not be here. Don't want to spend time in juvie when I go back to Minneapolis.

"You want to go for a walk, Sara?"

"Sure."

We walk along the beach. Feet in the water.

"I want to tell you about something." I hold her hand.

"You don't have to say it. I already know."

"You do?"

"Liam. I've been around summer guys my whole life."

"So?"

"You're going to tell me that you like hanging out with me, but you've got a girlfriend at home, right?"

Bust out laughing.

"That's funny?"

"No. I'm laughing at me. I don't have a girlfriend at home."

She moves closer to me. "Really?"

I kiss Sara for the first time. "Really." She kisses me back.

I'll tell her about camp later.

ENJOYING AN ACTUAL DATE

Me and Sara.

Thanks to some money I made trimming trees for Hank's friend, I was finally able to ask Sara to a movie.

Now we're sitting outside the ice-cream place. Double scoop of raspberry chocolate chip for me. Banana split for her.

"Hey, what were you going to tell me about the other night?"

"What?" Love this ice cream.

"You said you wanted to tell me about something. But then we started making out."

I smile.

"*That* you remember," she says. And laughs.

"How could I forget?" I kiss her. "What do you think of Lake Michigan Academy of Fine Arts?"

"Nice. Best of the best."

I shrug. "Kat told me about a camp there. Not sure I want to go."

"Are you kidding me?" She sets her bowl down.

"What do you mean?"

"You should definitely do it, Liam."

Gang wannabes walk past. "STB. Don't forget it, son." They point at my tag.

She watches them continue down the sidewalk. "I thought you wanted to be an artist."

"Yeah. But I haven't made my decision about the camp."

"Why?"

"I don't know." Yes, I do. "Because I'm scared."

She holds my hand. "Of what?"

"Not being an artist."

ACCEPTING THAT TIMING IS EVERYTHING

I just read this quote by an artist named Jim Hodges:

"[Picasso] was an artist who was always restless, always putting challenges in front of himself: doing and undoing, building and destroying. I see Picasso . . . as someone who was phenomenally gifted and never satisfied."

That's the final thing I needed. I'm going to the arts camp.

Finally tell Kat my decision.

"I'm glad, Liam."

"Yeah, me too." I need to learn how to paint a mural.

"I'll let registration know right away. Camp starts in a week."

"Okay." Hopefully this'll turn out all right.

REQUESTING PERMISSION FROM MOM

To go to camp. Phone's ringing.

"Hello?"

"Hey, Fiona. It's me."

"Me who?"

"Liam."

"Oh. Are you still in jail?"

"No. Is Mom there?" Please let her be home.

"When did you get out of jail?"

"Let me talk to Mom."

"Just in case you want to know, I'm the only one of my friends who has two brothers who had to go to jail."

"Okay."

"It's embarrassing. Sheesh."

"Fiona?"

"What? Are you going to apologize for making me embarrassed?" she says.

"Nope."

"What, then?"

"Put Mom on the phone."

"MOM! Liam wants to talk to you. I don't think he's in jail this time, but I'm not sure."

"Liam?" Mom picks up. "Did something *else* happen?"

This is great. "No." Can hear Fiona laughing hysterically.

"Just a minute, Liam. Fiona! That's not funny." Sighs. "So how are you, honey?"

"Fine. I was wondering if you'd give me permission to go to the arts camp where Kat teaches."

"Arts camp?"

"Yeah, a camp for kids who are artists. Remember you told me about it?"

"Yes, I remember the camp. I'm just pleasantly surprised that you want to go."

"Kat's getting me registered. I need your permission."

"How much is it?"

"Free. She's on the faculty."

"Oh. Right."

Silence.

"Mom?"

"Sure. You have my permission. When is it?"

"July seventeenth through the thirty-first."

"Wow, that's . . ."

"Five days from now."

"I'm really happy that you want to go. I know that you'll do great."

"Thanks. Kat said that she'll call you tomorrow with all the details."

"I only work in the afternoon tomorrow. So she can call me in the morning. Wait, I have to go to Kieran's preliminary hearing in the morning, but I'll be home for lunch."

"What's going on with Kieran?"

"Not much. We met with his public defender last week. It's going to be a while before his actual trial. I guess that's not bad, though. The Los Crooks guy who pulled the gun on you is already in prison."

"Really? How?"

"He had other outstanding felony warrants. I heard he got a twenty-year sentence."

"Oh." Thank God. Maybe I won't have nightmares about him anymore.

"Everything's okay with you?"

"I'm good." Honestly.

"Did you finish your community service?"

"Yes."

"Okay. Well, I've got to get to the garden. Need to get the beans and raspberries picked. Tomatoes, too."

"Tomatoes? It's early."

"I know, but the plants are already covered with ripe cherry tomatoes."

"Hmmm." Love those things.

"At this rate, who knows what'll be ready to harvest when you get home in August."

"Probably the pumpkins."

"Right." She laughs. "I'll talk to you later, then?"

"Sure."

HOPING TO SEE SARA

She's working at the bakery. Bowzer's sleeping under the tree. Surrounded by a crowd of tourists.

"Hey, buddy. You're a great dog." I scratch behind his ears. Tail thumps on the sidewalk. "I've got something to give Sara. Sketched something special for her. I'll be back out later."

More commotion inside. Sara waves from behind the counter. My whole body takes a deep relaxing breath. Wait at the end of the long line. Leave for camp tomorrow morning. I'll miss her.

"May I get you something, gent?" She uses a fake British accent.

I do the same. "Actually I have something for you, lady." Tyrell and Sean would bust out laughing if they heard me talking like this. Hand her a page from my blackbook. Rolled and tied with twine.

"Liam." She carefully removes the tie. Unrolls the sketch. "Liam, this is beautiful."

"Your very own coast guard cutter."

"It looks so real," she says. "This is really great."

"Thanks. You've got your boat. Now you *have* to be a Coastie."

She hurries around the counter. Hugs me like she means it. "You're an amazing artist. Thank you."

"You're welcome. See you in two weeks."

"Oh." Her smile disappears. "I thought you were driving back and forth every day."

"We are, but we have to leave by eight every morning and we won't get home until late." I hug her. "But I'll think about you all the time."

She laughs. "That's probably not a good idea. Shouldn't your brain be filled with creative thoughts?"

"I don't know. Maybe you're my muse."

"Right." She tilts her head to the side. "Are you messing with me, Liam O'Malley?"

"Seriously. All the great artists have a muse. Picasso definitely. And Basquiat." At least I think so.

SHAKING A CAN OF SPRAY PAINT AT ARTS CAMP

CLIKCLAKCLIKCLAKCLIKCLAK. Love this sound. Looking at the label. Molotow Premium. Of course. What all the pros use. I'm not a pro. Cliff Green. Green signifies new life in Catholicism. Stomach queasy. Push down on the nozzle.

Wait.

Not sure about this. But we have to show an example of our work. First class of the first day at camp. Other students are standing in front of their easels. Using paint. Charcoal. Pencils to do their thing. I feel all alone in this crowded room. Graffiti is my *thing*. All I know right now. What if this piece is crap?

CLIKCLAKCLIKCLAKCLIKCLAK. Push down on the nozzle. Spray.

Not yet.

Never done this in the light of day. Never in front of anyone else. Especially not at an academy of arts. Standing in a painting studio. Staring at a white canvas. Not a concrete wall this time. Visual arts students. Teachers. Do they know I don't belong here? C'mon, O'Malley. Now.

PSSSSSSSSSSSSSSSSSSSSSSSSSST.

Feeling like everyone is watching me. I'm watching the

Cliff Green invading the white surface. Doing a new piece I've been practicing in my blackbook. Pretending it's just the can and me. Graffiti writing is a solitary art. Painting my piece. Introducing my work.

TRYING.

OPENING MY ARTIST TOOLBOX

Every visual arts camper got one. Feeling like a little kid on Christmas morning. Checking items off the list.

1 angular watercolor brush
1 angular acrylic brush
1 bright acrylic brush
1 flat all-media brush
Set of 15 soft pastel sticks
Set of 12 studio drawing pencils (6B through 6H)
Set of studio colored pencils
Set of basic ceramic tools
Pack of 8 Sharpie fine point markers
1 Sharpie Magnum 44 marker
1 flash drive for digital storage

Very cool. No. Exceedingly cool.

LEARNING HOW TO BE AN ARTIST

Studying the masters of painting. I already know most of them from Kat's books.

We look at slide after slide after slide of old stuff.

I almost fall asleep. This feels like school.

"Study and learn." The teacher keeps clicking the humming projector.

Okay. But my favorite work isn't hanging on a perfect wall in some fancy gallery.

She turns on the lights. "Now, let's talk about what we just saw."

Hands fly up.

Teacher claps. "Let me hear. No hands necessary."

Everyone starts talking.

"Impressionism."

"Symbolism."

"Renaissance."

"Fauvism."

"Constructivism."

"Where're the contemporary paintings?" Can't believe I said that.

She looks at me. "Contemporary?"

I nod.

"Did you have a specific artist in mind, um . . . ?"

"Liam."

"Were you looking for someone in particular, Liam?"

"Jean-Michel Basquiat?"

Everyone turns and stares. Somebody laughs.

Feel like I'm back at Saint Al's.

HIDING IN KAT'S STUDIO

Told her I was sick. Couldn't go to camp today.
    Not going back. Not after feeling like a fool yesterday.
    Send my ship out, huh, Kat?
    Right.

"I'm not like them."

"What are you talking about?" Kat shoves tubes of paint out of the way. Sits on the table.

"The kids at arts camp."

She shakes her head. "Why would you want to be?"

"I don't know any of the terms they used in Masters of Painting yesterday."

"Like what?"

"Fauvism, Constructivism, other stuff."

"Big deal."

"It is for me, Kat."

"You can easily learn terms. What you already know instinctively about creating art—most of them will never be able to learn that."

"So?"

"So get over it and move on."

"Nice attitude, Kat."

"Listen. You think you're the only kid that's been given the short end of the stick, Liam? Come on. Plenty of kids have dads who are drunks. And maybe even older brothers who make dangerous decisions. But they don't give up. You know? They don't just sit around feeling sorry for themselves."

"That's not what I'm doing." Am I?

She shrugs.

I don't want to be here. "It's not that."

"Then maybe you should figure out what *it* is and stop throwing away your chances." She walks out of the studio.

I'm so tired of hearing crap like that from everyone. Kat said she's not my mom. She sure sounds like it now.

TRANSITIONING FROM TAGGER TO ARTIST

Going from wall to canvas like Jean-Michel Basquiat?

That's what I'm supposedly trying to do at arts camp. Maybe. Maybe not. But I'm back here anyway. On the shore of Lake Michigan. Campus used to be an old US Lifesaving Station. Wonder if Sara knows that's how the coast guard started.

First class of the morning is Painting Aesthetics. Teacher explains the characteristics of oil-and-water-based media. We get to work with whatever type of paint we want. A stack of canvases on the corner of my table. Intimidating.

Tell the guy next to me, "I've only really been using Sharpies or spray paint."

"Usually watercolors for me. But it'd be decent to try something with acrylics."

He's from Los Angeles. Nice to meet kids who are into art. Just like me.

The teacher walks around the studio while he talks. Encourages us to create imagery that showcases our personal concepts and ideas. Tells us to embrace our strengths so that our work will become more mature and developed.

Learning to develop my own concepts and ideas. Hard to do here in this beautiful classroom. My aesthetic is

grounded in street art. Gritty. Loud. Connected to the city.
I get ideas by observing what's around me. What's real.
Struggling with what it means to be an art student. Studying the work of the masters. Okay. But my favorite work
isn't hanging on a perfect wall in some fancy gallery. Want
my art to be open to the public. On some alley wall in the
hood. Possible? Is that a real artist?

Maybe.

More mature and developed? I'm working on it.

My mind's ready to explode.

PAYING ATTENTION TO KAT, AKA MS. SULLIVAN

I'm in her Beginning Sculpture class.

We study the sculptural processes of addition, subtraction, manipulation, and substitution. She tells us to move out of our comfort zone.

"I'd like to move closer to her comfort zone." Painter from LA elbows me.

"What?"

"She's hot."

Never thought of her that way. I don't look at him. Or Kat.

"Are you blind?"

"Whatever." Don't want him to know I live with Kat. "That's your opinion."

"Guys?" She points to the whiteboard. "You understand all of this?"

Silence.

"Pay attention, then. You don't want to miss anything."

"I totally agree with you, Ms. Sullivan." He smirks.

I shake my head. "Get your mind back on sculpture, man."

"Okay. Time to do some work in your sketchbooks," Kat says. "I want you to incorporate what we've been discussing this morning into an idea that'll translate into clay. I'll walk around and take a look at your sketches. They need to be clear and complete."

All the teachers here stress the importance of being able to work proficiently in our sketchbooks. Kat says it's vital to our development as visual artists.

I already know.

My blackbook has been my only teacher until coming to this camp.

INVESTIGATING THE MEANING OF COLORS

Thinking about how they can communicate mood and emotion. That's what I tried to do by using Midnight Black, Shock Blue, and Tornado Red on my bathhouse piece. Guess I knew something about colors without having to learn it from someone else. But I'll take notes anyway.

Red = excitement, ambition, impulsiveness

Orange = assertive, dynamic, fearlessness

Yellow = hope, wisdom, happiness

Green = harmony, security, peace

Blue = openness, wisdom, masculine

Purple = dignity, restfulness, wit

Brown = restfulness, dependability, conscientiousness

Gray = caution, compromise, sense of peace

White = safety, perfection, innocence

Black = dignity, mystery, hiddenness

Everything I'm learning is useful. Helps me to think like a painter.

Like an artist.

GOOFING AROUND

It's free time. Going to play Ultimate Frisbee. Do something physical for a change. Usually we just keep talking shop. Waiting with a guy from one of my classes. He's a printmaker.

"With a name like O'Malley, you have to be Irish," he says. He has an accent.

"Yep. Are you from Ireland?"

"Belfast." He pounds his heart with his fist.

"Wow, Belfast. Pretty violent, huh?"

"It was during the Troubles. Not so much now."

"Are you Catholic or Protestant?"

"Let's just say that I'm a huge University of Notre Dame fan."

"Cool. Me too," I say.

"And I have this." He pulls a Saint Patrick holy medal out from under his shirt.

"Ha!" I do the same with my Saint Brendan medal. "Good Catholic boys, right?"

We bump fists.

A bunch of other guys join us. Enough for two Frisbee teams. We head over to the field. Pass a group of girls on the way.

They wave. "Hey, guys."

"Dudes. The girls are checking us out," someone says.

"Hi, Liam." A dancer says. Waves.

Another guy shoves me. "She likes you, *Liiiiiiiaaaaaaam.*"

Everyone laughs. Including me. She's beautiful and . . . so is Sara. I keep walking.

"What are you doing, man? That dancer's flirting with you. You're dissing her."

I wave back.

Painter from LA looks at me. "That's it, O'Malley?"

"Yep." I think of Sara's smile. "I have a girlfriend."

"Damn. I'd be all over that." He shakes his head.

"What? And cheat on Ms. Sullivan?"

He starts dancing. "In a heartbeat, bro!"

Kid's a clown. Can't help but laugh.

TROUBLING MY MIND

Worrying about art stuff. Trying to sleep. Hoping the sound of the waves will help me relax.

Camp will be done in a couple of days. It's been incredible but also stressful. Been bombarded with so many things. Words race through my mind constantly. *Form. Volume. Plane. Line. Space. Texture. Surface. Oil. Acrylic. Watercolor.* Things swirl together like an abstract painting. What if I forget everything I've learned?

Painting teacher told me about a graffiti-mentoring program in Minneapolis. Said I should check it out when I get home. Don't even have time to think about that.

And all the teachers emphasize the *importance of bringing contemporary and traditional art aesthetics into our studio sessions.*

What the . . . ? Does that mean I have to move from street to studio with my work? Can I still be a graffiti writer and be considered a visual artist?

The work I love to create shows my aesthetic to everyone. Out in public anytime and anyplace.

Then there's all of the drawing, drawing, drawing. And then drawing some more.

I'm almost sick of my blackbook. Almost.

DEFYING EXPECTATIONS

Eating lunch and discussing street art. It's me, the print-maker from Belfast, the painter from LA, and a few other guys. Group of girls at the table next to us. We try not to pay attention to them.

"Seriously, Liam. You should come to Northern Ireland some time and see all the murals. There're more than two thousand."

"Awesome." That would be cool to go to my motherland. "Were they all created by Catholics?"

"Catholics and Protestants. Most were painted during the Troubles in the 1970s."

"Sounds like the gang murals in LA," the painter says. "A lot of times they use murals to mark their territory."

"Gangs do that in Minneapolis, too," I say. Haven't thought about Irish Mafia or Los Crooks lately. "But there're some other really decent pieces and murals. Created by local graffiti writers."

"A lot of the murals in my Belfast neighborhood were put up to make political statements. They used art to force Catholic or Protestant issues instead of guns and bombs."

"That's cool." Maybe I could make social statements with my work.

The girls are laughing.

"Man, I just don't understand girls. Not in Ireland and not here in the States."

"Me either," painter says. "That's why I want to be with a *woman*."

"Don't even say it . . ." I shake my head.

"*Ms. Sullivan.* Hear her name and weep for your loss, boys."

We laugh.

"You've got a girlfriend, Liam. School us on all that stuff."

"Nope." I miss Sara. "I don't kiss and tell."

Painter from LA grabs his heart. Pretends he's dying.

We've become pretty good friends the past couple of weeks. A crew. Like me, Tyrell, and Sean. Going to miss my artist friends like I miss my hood friends.

LEAVING LAKE MICHIGAN
ACADEMY OF FINE ARTS

Riding shotgun in the Rover.

Heading back to Lakeshore. Camp is officially over.

"So, what did you think?" Kat says.

"It was okay."

"Oh, c'mon."

"Okay. Very cool."

"Were you inspired?"

"Someday I want to paint something like *Guernica*."

"Picasso was brilliant, wasn't he?" She sighs.

"I've been studying his techniques."

"He was such a brave artist. Always reinventing himself."

"That's one of the things I like best about him."

She nods.

Driving along the shore. Lake Michigan's sparkling like broken glass in an alley. Peaceful.

"I'd like to paint a mural." Look at Kat out of the corner of my eye.

"That would be great. Especially with your, *ahem*, varied experiences."

"I've been working on something in my blackbook."

"I'd love to see it."

"Okay." Thinking about what I've learned at camp. "I feel like I could actually do one."

"I've watched your work grow exponentially during the past two weeks, Liam. I know that you can paint a mural."

Nod.

"Where are you going to paint it? Minneapolis?"

"I was thinking about Lakeshore."

"Really?"

"I'd like to find a big wall near the lake," I say.

"Liam . . ."

"Don't worry." Try not to laugh.

"Oh . . . I wasn't worried. I . . ."

"I'm just kidding."

Kat smiles. "Very funny, smart-ass."

We laugh.

RESEARCHING EMPTY WALLS

Looking around. Checking different wall sizes. Trying to get ideas for my sketches. Walk up and down Main Street with Sara and Bowzer. Eat cherry muffins from the bakery. Nice to be able to spend the day in town again. Snake around a bunch of tourists. Crowd outside the ice-cream place.

Hank walks out. "What's your hurry?" He has a double-scoop chocolate.

I shake his hand.

"Haven't seen you around lately, Liam."

"I was at art camp for two weeks." It's nice to see him.

"Yessir. That's right. Been kind of quiet here. Wouldn't ya say, Sara?" He winks.

"It has." She squeezes my hand.

Dying to kiss her.

Hank clears his throat. "So where're you headed?"

"Just looking at empty walls. Trying to find one that's as big as one of my favorite paintings."

He looks at me. Lifts an eyebrow.

"Needs to be twenty-five feet wide and twelve feet tall."

He stares.

"For research." Sara says. She's got my back.

Nod. "It's all good, Hank."

DIALING 612

Want to tell Mom how cool camp was. Hope she doesn't talk too much.

"Hello?" Patrick answers.

"Hey, what's up?"

"Liam. Um. How's it going, man?"

"Okay. You?"

"It's all good in the hood."

He's talking weird. "What's going on around the JFKs?"

"You know. A little of this and a little of that."

What's with all the gang slang? "Where's Mom?"

"She took the little kids to the library."

"When will they be home?"

"Yo, Paddy-Boy!" I hear a guy's voice in the background. "Let's go, man. We've got things to do."

Paddy-Boy? "Who's that, Patrick?" Voice sounds familiar.

"What? Oh, ah . . . just a friend."

"Who?" Patrick's nervous. I can hear it in his voice.

"What do you mean?

"Who's there at the apartment with you?" Doesn't sound like any of his friends. But still familiar.

"Ahhh. It's, ummm. It's . . ."

"Give me the phone, shorty." It's a guy's muffled voice.

"Hello? Who wants to know?"

"Who is this?" I know that voice. Tommy? Irish Mafia loser?

"You first, man."

"Liam."

"Well, well, well, if it isn't little mister boojie-ass himself. Summering at the lake. Don't tell me you miss the hood already."

Crap. "What are you doing there, Tommy?"

"Paddy-Boy invited me. What's it to you?"

"Put Patrick back on." He shouldn't be hanging with Kieran's gang. What's going on? "Give the phone to my brother."

"I don't think he wants to talk to you. Besides, we're busy."

"Put Patrick on!" I've got to tell him not to mess with Irish Mafia.

"What?" Patrick's back.

"What are you doing? Stay away from him. I'm not fooling around. Tell him you've got to do something. Make something up. Get him out of our apartment."

"Our apartment? Last time I checked you didn't live here anymore, Liam."

"Tommy bangs with Irish Mafia. He's a corner boy."

"Why do you care?"

"What's your problem, Patrick?"

"You probably already forgot what it's like, man. You

don't have to walk past Los Crooks every day. They know I'm an O'Malley. Look what happened to Kieran. They're going to beat the *crap* out of me. Maybe worse."

"What don't you get? Stop hanging with Irish Mafia!" But I know that he needs the protection. "You can go to the cops. Let them know what's going on. Maybe they could—"

"Right. Like they're going to do anything. They're too busy busting guys on petty drug charges."

"Give me the phone, Paddy-Boy." It's Tommy again. "Hey, Liam, go back to your beach chair, man. I've got your brother's back."

Click.

CIRCLING THE LIVING ROOM

Dialing our home number again. *Ring. Ring. Ring.*

Pick up the phone, Patrick.

Hanging up. Mind racing. Paddy-Boy? This cannot be happening. How can he be so stupid? We've talked about how dangerous it is to hang out with Kieran's gang. Now look. I'm hundreds of miles away. Can't even help him. Why did Mom send me here?

"SHITE!"

Dialing. Ringing. He's only twelve. Doesn't know enough about the streets. He's by himself. No one is there in Minneapolis to look out for him, because I got myself sent here.

Dialing again. *Ring. Ring. Ring.* No answer.

Need to get out of here.

Run.

Into the studio.

Pacing, pacing, pacing.

"NOOOOOOOOOOOOOOOOO!"

Grab a bunch of colored pencils in my right hand. Handful of paper in my left. Out the door. But I don't run. Walk down to the beach. Then along the concrete breakwater out to the lighthouse. Climb up the ladder to the walkway around the huge light. Find the perfect spot. Sit. Breathe.

Love the view from up here.

Can see all around Lakeshore. Kat's house. Studio. Beach-volleyball courts. Coast guard station. Main Street. Bakery. Hardware store. Theater. Saint Catherine's Church. Sara's house. Library. Hank's house. Harbor. My favorite sailboat. Town hall. Baseball fields at the park. Road to Lake Michigan Academy of Fine Arts.

Pieces of my summer. Everything that surrounds me. Like a beautiful painting.

Open my blackbook. Need to sketch what's in front of me. What's been surrounding me the past couple of months. Being in the little town of Lakeshore *has* been good for me. Wish Patrick could escape to this peaceful place, too.

As angry as I am at him, I know he would love it up here and down there.

Graphite pencil in hand. Scrapes across the paper. I sketch this peaceful scene.

SWIMMING IN LINES

Back and forth. Fifty feet offshore. Straight out from Kat's. Early morning water's warm. Calm. Easy to move through. Back and forth. Yesterday was stressful because of that crap with Patrick. But today I keep going. Keep thinking. Have to figure out how to help my brother. If he's hanging out with Tommy, he might be banging with Irish Mafia.

One arm in front of the other. Left. Right. Left. Right. Keep moving. Got to clear my head. Calm down. Think straight.

Decide to send my latest sketch to Patrick straightaway. Know it's not much but maybe it'll help him remember that he's not alone.

Need to keep him out of the wreck.

ILLUMINATING THE FACE OF MARY

At Saint Catherine's Church. Kneel in front of the grotto. The statue of Our Lady of Perpetual Help looks down at me. Arms out at her sides. Palms up like she's saying: What now?

My stomach's been in knots off and on for a few days.

I pray the Hail Mary. For Patrick. What can I do from here? Being in Lakeshore has been a good thing. But it's like I've abandoned Patrick and the little kids, too.

"Keep all of them safe. Please help me know what I'm supposed to be doing." I light a candle directly below Mary. Look at her bare feet. She stands on a snake's head. Keeping evil away.

LONGING TO BE ALONE IN THE STUDIO

Want to be surrounded by art. Alone with my thoughts. I walk in the door.

"Hi." Kat pulls some tools out of a cloth bag.

"Hey." Love this place. Would give anything to have a studio like this someday. "Hope it's okay if I came out here."

"I think you know my answer." She smiles. "Mind if I do some work?"

"It's your studio." She's working on a complicated metal sculpture. She was working on it when I got to Lakeshore. It looks exactly the same as it did two months ago.

"Great news! I had an epiphany about my sculpture this afternoon."

"A new idea?" Stacks of metal on the table. I stare at pieces of me in the reflections.

"More like a revision of an old idea. I want to get started straightaway and see what happens."

"How do you come up with new ideas all the time?" I say.

"I'm not sure. I just know that I have to try different things so I don't get bogged down."

Nod.

"I think of it as traveling light, you know? That way I can keep moving," she says.

"Hmmm." I watch her work. She looks at her sketch. Grabs the calipers.

What way should I keep moving? Can't stop thinking of Patrick back home.

PHONING MINNEAPOLIS AGAIN

"Hi, Mom."

"Liam. How are things in Lakeshore?"

"Good."

"Really?"

"Yeah. Where's Patrick?"

"He's . . . at the park? I think."

"Are you sure?" I don't want to worry her.

"I'm more than a little busy, Liam. Two jobs, single parent, five kids . . ."

"I know."

"Hang on," she says. "Patrick?" I hear mumbling. "He's in the shower. He just got home from soccer practice at the park. Okay?"

"Yeah." Feel relieved. "Tell him to look for something from me in the mail, okay?"

"Sure. How was arts camp?"

"Great. I learned a lot."

"Did you make some new friends?"

"Yeah. Bunch of artists."

"Were they all painters?"

"Some were. Everyone was cool."

"I'm glad that you had the opportunity to go."

"Well, I've got some work to do. I guess I better go."

"Work?"

"Sketching. A new idea."

"No more graffiti?"

"Just trying different things."

"Not graffiti, right?"

Give me a chance. "It's for a mural," I say.

"Mural?"

"Here in Lakeshore."

"Wow."

"Yeah. I want to do something for the town. Like restitution."

"As a way to make things right?"

"Yes. And to say thanks." That thought just came to me.

"That's wonderful, Liam," she says.

"I'm going to make a proposal for the town council." I still can't believe I even thought about doing this.

"I'm proud of you. Let me know what happens."

"I will."

"Good. Thanks for calling. It's nice to hear that things are going great for you."

"Okay. Talk to you later." I'll phone back in a day or two. To check on Patrick again.

"I love you, Liam."

"I know."

WORKING ON MY CREATION

Moving from *vandalistic* tags and pieces to *artistic* murals.

But still creating something for everyone to see. My way to tell a story in public. A chance to get my work seen by people who might never go into an art gallery.

Been sketching ideas in my blackbook. Messing around with things I saw from the lighthouse the other day. Have to think big.

Studied muralists at arts camp. Love the work of Diego Rivera. He painted the amazing mural *Detroit Industry* in 1933. It's one of his most famous pieces. Still on the walls of the Detroit Institute of Arts. Kat and I talked about going to see it later in August. I like his attention to detail. But his style was more futuristic and about social realism. A style that would fit better in a big city like Minneapolis.

I'll create my mural using abstract expressionism. Like Picasso's *Guernica*. Art that's abstract but also makes you feel something emotionally. Picasso and Rivera created murals to use as social and political tools. Forced people to think in different ways. Just like graffiti writers.

Now it's my turn. And my style.

A mural for Lakeshore. Inspired by Lakeshore. With permission from Lakeshore. I hope the town council goes for it.

Doing something here will give me a chance to practice. That way I won't fail miserably when I try to create a mural in my hood.

Perfect.

APPROACHING TOWN HALL

I'm early. Better than late. Heart pounding. Kat gave me a tie to wear. Wish she were here. Got to do this myself if I want to have any chance to paint my mural.

"May I help you, young man?" a woman says. She looks exactly like our neighbor Mrs. Murphy in Minneapolis. Maybe I should ask her for a cigarette.

"I'm here for a meeting."

"With?"

"The town council."

"Let me check today's schedule."

Wait.

"Are you Liam O'Malley?"

"Yes."

"Looks like you'll be meeting in Room 101. Down the hall, second door on the right."

"Thank you." Looking for the room. 101. Hear a commotion.

"Why are we even thinking about letting an out-of-towner—a criminal—do something like this?"

Did the meeting already start? I'm late. Loud voices. Definitely coming from Room 101. Great. Already talking about me. This will not go well. I want to leave and go back to

Kat's. No. Chest tightens. Tug on my holy medal and whisper, "Saint Brendan, pray for me."

A man walks out of the room. "Are you here about the mural?"

"Yes."

"Liam?"

Nod. "O'Malley." Shake his hand.

"Come on in. We're just waiting for a few more people."

I enter a conference room with a big oblong table in the middle. People already seated. Hank salutes from the far end. Two other men and three women are scattered around the sides. Where am I supposed to sit?

"This is Liam O'Malley."

Silence.

"Let's wait for the others to get here before we do introductions."

All stare at me. Check my fingernails.

"Have a seat right here, Liam," the man from the hall says. "You brought a sketch of your proposal?"

"Yes."

Last four members of the town council wander in. Everyone introduces themselves. Meeting officially begins.

"I'm going to ask again," says a woman wearing a *Lakeshore Is for Lovers* sweatshirt. "Why are we considering letting a summer resident do this?"

"Graffiti isn't art; it's a crime," a man in a button-down shirt says.

I look down at my fingernails.

"We don't even know who this young man is," another says.

Forget this. Stupid to think that I might stand a chance.

"I'm sorry. Why don't we listen to Lenny's proposal," a woman says.

Enough. I want to quit.

"Liam, the floor's yours." Hank speaks up.

What's the point?

I feel like I've swallowed a golf ball again. I use magnets to attach my sketch to the whiteboard. Wanted to let my artwork do the talking. Walk over to the podium. We had to give artist-statement presentations at camp. But this isn't a group of fellow artists.

"Thanks for agreeing to listen to my idea," I say. Hate this. "I've been living with Katherine Sullivan this summer. I've met some decent people here in Lakeshore. When I first got to Lakeshore, I committed a crime. I painted a graffiti piece on your property." I think about how it did bring some energy to this boring little town, though.

"I'm sorry," I continue. "Since then, I've made the decision to better myself. So I went to camp at Lake Michigan Academy of Fine Arts where I studied the visual arts for two weeks. I discovered that I'm very interested in murals like Diego Rivera and Pablo Picasso created. I'd like to have the opportunity to paint a mural for the community of Lakeshore as restitution. I'd like to show you that I can do something decent."

Too much talking.

ASSISTING KAT

We move the base of her revised sculpture out of the studio. I'm trying to stay busy. Waiting to hear back from the town council.

"Dammit, this is heavy. Stop for a minute." Kat sets her end down.

"Where're we going to put this?"

"Over there." She points toward the old oak in the backyard. "See how the sunlight hits the ground between the big trees?"

"Very cool."

"The metal waves will really reflect the sun in that spot."

"Why not the front yard? On the sand. Sun shines all day out there."

"I like the play between light and dark," she says. "Good and bad."

"Yeah, I guess." I'd still put it in the front yard.

"Okay. Let's give it another try."

I lift my side. Heavy. Glad the backyard is closer.

"Thank God you're here, Liam."

DAYDREAMING OF GUERNICA

Massive.

Dark colors.

Cubism.

Powerful.

Serious.

Anger.

Danger.

Violence.

Distress.

Panic.

Death.

Patrick.

SHOUTING AT THE DOOR

"Liam!" Hank's on Kat's porch. "You home?"

"Yeah!" I go to the door.

"Can ya give me a hand, Liam?"

What now? "Sure." Helped him unload a shipment yesterday. All day.

"Got something that needs getting done. You're the man for the job."

"Okay." No big deal.

We walk down Kat's sand-covered street. Talk about the weather. Past the public beach and the boring white wall on the bathhouse. To the movie theater. Stop at the sidewall.

"How big do you think this wall is, Liam?"

"I don't know."

"It's exactly fourteen feet high and twenty-eight feet wide."

And? "Hmmm."

"The council met again," Hank says.

What's this have to do with me? What needs getting done?

"This wall will probably work just fine don't ya think?"

"Hank. I really don't know what you're talking about."

"Think you could paint something decent on this wall?"

"Wait a minute . . . You mean . . ."

"Yessir, Liam."

"No way."

"It's true. Lakeshore wants a community mural. And they decided to let you be the one to make it."

STARING AT MY CANVAS

My sidewall.

No bandanna tied around my mouth and nose. No hoodie covering my head. Daytime. Just me and this wall.

Empty. Waiting for my creation. To see what I have to say.

Blackbook out of my backpack. Checking my revisions. Happy with the final sketch. Vision is crystal clear. Scene. Colors. Emotions. True and beautiful. Modernism and my own style.

Shadows move over the sidewalk.

"Yo." Gang wannabes walk up.

What now? "Yeah?"

"What're you painting, man? You doing community service again or something?" They laugh. "Where's your neon vest, homeboy?"

"I'm just doing my job."

"Like painting houses and buildings and *walls*?"

"Right."

"What happens if we decide to do a graffiti thing on your wall? STB, man." They throw up their lame sign for Bloods.

"First, after you get arrested for vandalism, I guess I'll be laughing at your neon-vest-wearing sorry selves cleaning this wall."

They stare.

"Then me and my homies will kick your small-town asses for ruining my mural."

"No problem, man." They walk away. "It's all good."

Back to work.

STANDING IN THE KITCHEN

Reading the newest note on the fridge:

"I am for an art that takes its form from the lines of life itself, that twists and extends and accumulates and spits and drips, and is heavy and coarse and blunt and sweet and stupid as life itself." (Claes Oldenburg)

Bust out laughing.

Kat smiles. "Appropriate?"

"Yes. But why only quotes by Oldenburg?"

"Oh, I don't know. I guess because I love his pop art sculptures and his moxie."

"Makes sense." Not pop art, though. I don't personally care much about paintings of soup cans and cartoons. But it is someone's aesthetic, so I stay respectful. "What kind of sculptures?"

"Oldenburg started out using materials he found on the street in NYC. Like cardboard and paint from cans people put out with the garbage."

"So he made art in the middle of garbage? Sounds like a street artist."

"Exactly. He moved on to creating soft sculptures in studios later, but I appreciate his beginnings."

"Yeah, that's a great story." Maybe Oldenburg is okay.

"How's your mural coming along?" She opens the fridge.

"Good."

Throws me a pear. "How much longer until you'll be finished?"

"Four or five days."

"Can't wait to see it." She grabs a handful of blueberries. "I've been staying away until you're done."

"Want to see it so far?" I say.

"Let's go!"

REVEALING MY AESTHETIC

Walk down Main Street with Kat. We're quiet all the way to the theater.

Pull the cloth off the scaffolding.

Silence.

"Liam . . . what you've done so far is amazing." Kat moves closer to the wall. "Powerful. Disciplined." She takes a few steps back. "Cubism." She stares. "Aggressive and bold, yet sensitive. Abstract expressionism. Filled with spontaneous energy." I see tears in her eyes.

She looks at me.

I look away.

"Your work is truly brilliant. I mean it, Liam."

"Thank you."

Silence. Not awkward.

"This may not be the right time. Maybe it's the perfect time."

"What?"

"Would you ever consider going to the boarding school at Lake Michigan?"

"What?" What did she just say?

"Lake Michigan Academy of Fine Arts. Attending the fine-arts high school."

"Are you kidding me?" Wait. Be real, O'Malley. "I could never afford to go."

"There are scholarships."

"What would I need to do?"

"Complete the application and get your portfolio together."

"I don't have a portfolio."

"What about this mural?" she says.

"All right."

"And the excellent work you created at camp."

I nod.

"And your sketchbook."

"My blackbook?"

"Good God, Liam! Yes, your *blackbook*."

We laugh.

"I want you to give the boarding school some serious thought. Admissions might still be open for the new school year. But you'd have to get your application submitted right away."

"Okay."

"I mean it. You're very talented."

I want to believe Kat. "Thanks," I say.

Very talented? Truly brilliant? Warm waves roll through my whole body.

I'm smiling the biggest damn smile of my whole life.

DELAYING MY APPLICATION

Can't move forward until I talk to Patrick. Need to find out about Irish Mafia. I dial our number.

"Hello?"

"Hey, Patrick."

"What's up, Liam?"

"Are you still hanging out with Tommy?" I say.

"What do you care, man?"

"Knock it off. You know what I'm talking about. He's a loser."

"I'm kidding." He laughs. "I don't even like the guy. Why would I be around him?"

"You were when I phoned before."

"That was a couple of weeks ago, Liam. Things can change over time, you know?

"I don't want you anywhere near that guy."

"Okay, *Dad*."

"Don't *ever* compare me to Dad." My hands are shaking. "Ever."

"All right. Sorry."

Take a deep breath. "Seriously, Patrick." I calm down. "Stay away from Irish Mafia."

"I'm not with them. I don't bang."

"You sure?" Patrick has never lied to me.

"Yeah. It's all good."

"Okay." He's never lied to me. I'm trying to believe him. "Oh, did you get the sketch I sent you?"

"Yeah. It's cool, Liam. It looks so real I almost feel like I'm there."

I wish he was. "Glad you like it."

"I have to go. Mom's making me help her at the garden."

"You all like to eat? Then you all have to help in the garden."

"She actually told me that." He laughs. "I swear to God."

We bust out laughing.

"Okay. Talk to you later, Patrick."

"Yeah, later."

ROCKING IN THE HAMMOCK
WITH SARA

We're side by side. Leaves in the huge oak trees are turning brown. I look out over the sand to the waves of Lake Michigan. They're darker blue now.

"Move over a little bit, Liam."

"I can't."

"You have to or we're going to flip."

"My back hurts."

"What happened?"

"I scraped it on one of those big boulders near the breakwater out to the lighthouse."

"Fine. I'll move." She carefully slides to the right. "*Baby.*"

"Thanks a lot." Love being with Sara.

We rock back and forth. Relaxing.

"That'd be great if you did go to the Academy of Arts." She smiles. "You'd be a lot closer than Minneapolis."

"Yeah." That'd be nice.

"Have you finished your application?"

"I'm almost done. Then I have to prepare my portfolio."

"What are you putting in it?"

"At least five examples of my finished work. Some of my stuff from camp. Pages from my blackbook. Kat said my portfolio needs to reflect my creative potential, process, and overall abilities."

"From what you've shown me, and even your piece on the bathhouse, I'd definitely say you're in."

We kiss. Not awkwardly anymore.

"I hope." Lean my head against hers. Comfortable.

Screen door creaks. Kat walks out onto the porch. "Dinner's ready. Come on in."

All the pieces are coming together.

CALLING MINNEAPOLIS

"Hello?" It's Fiona.

"Hey."

"Liam! Everybody, it's Liam." She shouts to whoever can hear. Declan yells my name.

"Fiona?" Did she walk away from the phone? "*Fiona?*"

"Let me talk to your brother," Mom says. "Then you and Declan can each have a turn."

"Liam?"

"Hi, Mom." We haven't talked in over a week. Been busy.

"Did you finish the mural?"

"Should be done in a couple of days."

"How does it look so far?"

"I'm happy with it."

"I'm very proud of you," she says.

"Thanks."

"I mean it, Liam."

"I know." Seriously.

"So . . . how's everything else in Lakeshore?"

"Good. What's going on with Kieran?" Been thinking about him.

"Nothing new. We're still waiting for his court date."

"Oh." He's been sitting in jail for most of the summer.

"How's the weather over there?"

"Nice. Remember the arts camp I went to?"

"Yes. Why?"

"Because they have a boarding school. I'd really like to apply for admission this fall. Kat thinks I should. I already filled out my application. I'm getting my portfolio together. And I can probably get a scholarship to pay for all of my tuition. And room and board. Since we don't have a lot of money."

"Liam . . . honey . . . Kat and I have already talked. She went through all of the details."

"Oh." Pressure's off me. "Okay."

"You're sure this is something you want to do? Because you thought Saint Al's was, and look how that turned out."

"Mom."

"I'm not trying to discourage you. I'm just nervous about all of this."

"But this is Lake Michigan Academy of Fine Arts."

"You'd be living there for the whole school year. I don't even know if I'd have the money to fly you home for holidays."

"I could stay at Kat's during breaks," I say.

"Patrick, Fiona, and Declan would sure miss you."

"I know. But I really want to do this."

Silence.

"Mom?"

"Boarding school is a big step, Liam. *I'd* miss you."

"I'd probably miss you guys, too. But you did want me to make big changes this summer."

"I did, and I know that you're trying."

"That's why this is so important to me. I don't want to throw away my chance." Please say yes.

"Okay, then. You have my permission to submit the application."

"Very cool!"

"Good luck."

"Thank you."

"Well, Fiona and Declan want to talk to you."

Their loud voices get closer.

"Liam." Declan clears his throat. "Liam, how are you doing in Lakeshore, Michigan? When are you coming home to Minneapolis, Minnesota?"

"I don't know."

"Give me the phone right now." Fiona snaps her fingers. "It's my turn to talk to Liam. I was talking first, even before Mom."

"No! Give me the phone back, Fiona."

"For the love of all the Irish saints," Mom says. "Quit yanking on that phone before you pull it right out of the—"

CRAAAASH.

Click.

PLEADING FOR REDEMPTION

Please, God.

My Lake Michigan Academy of Fine Arts application is in the mailbox. I tug on my holy medal for good luck. Again. Surprised the chain hasn't broken yet. "Saint Brendan, pray for me." Start down the sidewalk. Head home. I mean, head to Kat's.

Home?

BARING MY SOUL

Surrounded by people of this *Welcome to Lakeshore!* little town. Kat. Hank. Librarian. Gang wannabes. Sara's mom. Town council members. Local kids. Cop who arrested me. Everyone. I tug on my holy medal.

I'm standing beside Sara, next to my covered mural. Heart's racing. Listening to the mayor talk about the community vision of Lakeshore. About the importance of art in the life of a community.

Thinking about the importance of art in the life of me.

Mayor raises his voice. "And now, I'd like to present the very talented artist who created our wonderful mural: Liam O'Malley." Clapping. He shakes my hand. Hands me the microphone.

"I just want to say thanks to . . . ummm . . . I just want to say thanks to the town council for taking a chance on my work. And thanks especially to Kat, the Lady Artist, for taking a chance on me this summer."

Kat's crying. Feel like a golf ball's in my throat again.

"And to Sara and Hank, too." I walk over to the side of the scaffolding. Slow down. Pull the rope. The cover drops to the sidewalk. Revealing everything. The Lakeshore Community Mural. Everything I learned this summer. Me.

People take in their breath. I'm holding mine.

All sorts of voices start in. I don't want to see who's saying what. I just look at my work.

"Hey, the lighthouse is covered with faces."

"Scenes from Lakeshore are in different pieces."

"What a beautiful color of yellow for the beam of light."

"Cool. Check out the bits of graffiti in the stormy water."

"Is that Lakeshore written in the light coming from the lighthouse?"

Loud clapping and cheering. Cameras flash.

Sara hugs me. "It's absolutely amazing, Liam." She smiles her smile.

I breathe again.

FINISHING PROPERLY

It's late at night. I'm wearing my black hoodie and bandanna. Backpack's filled with supplies.

One thing left. Stand in front of the side wall of the theater. Lakeshore Community Mural. My way of saying thank you. Even in the dark.

Look all around. Pull the can out of my backpack.

CLIKCLAKCLIKCLAKCLIKCLAK. Plastic cap off. Look again. Now. Press down on the nozzle.

PSSSSSSSSSSSSSSSSSSSSSSSSSST.

Spraying over my old voice. Black paint and paint remover drips down from the bench. Forms a puddle on the sidewalk. Dump a bucket of water over the mess.

Getting rid of *St. B.* Already cleaned up the garbage can and the stop sign.

Tagged no more. At least in Lakeshore, where it's not considered art.

Take the gold Sharpie marker out of my backpack. Sign my mural:

Liam Brendan O'Malley

I am here.
I exist.

OPENING THE MAILBOX

Third time today.

Nothing yet.

Go back to reading *The Chocolate War*. I'm almost finished.

I know how Jerry felt. Like he was all alone at his Catholic school. He had trouble with his football teammates. Baseball teammates for me. I didn't get my ass kicked like Jerry, but I did have a Glock jabbed into the side of my head.

At least I won't be going back to Saint Al's.

Hopefully Jerry won't have to stay at Trinity.

HOLDING THE ENVELOPE

It's addressed to Liam Brendan O'Malley. From Lake Michigan Academy of Fine Arts. Need to open this somewhere else.

Walk down the beach. Knee-deep in the big lake. Carefully open the envelope.

Dear Liam:

Congratulations! We're pleased to accept you to Lake Michigan Academy of Fine Arts for the upcoming academic year. Our decision was based on the strong work in your Visual Arts portfolio, as well as the outstanding artistic recommendation from Katherine Sullivan and character recommendation from Clarence Masterson.

Our academy is a prominent fine-arts boarding school, recognized nationally and globally. You will be joining a strong community of artists who share your artistic and academic goals and dreams. We believe your high school experience at Lake Michigan Academy of Fine Arts will be like no other. Welcome!

Sincerely,

Joseph Konczal

Director of Admissions

"*Yes!*" Luck of the Irish.

Thank you, God. And thank you, Kat and Hank.

I resist the urge to dive in. Want to keep this letter. Forever.

REACHING TYRELL

"Liam. What's going on, man?"

"I'm good. How's the hood? You. Sean. Everyone?"

"Same old thing. Our baseball team's in first place. We should win the City Park League again this year."

"Very cool."

"Coach moved the lineup around. I'm batting cleanup since you're not here."

"Oh." That's my spot.

"We need you for the playoffs, though. When you home?"

Home. The JFKs. "I'm not sure." Feels like I left a lifetime ago. "How's Sean?"

"His sister and her kids moved back in. Four more people in his apartment."

"No."

"Guess where Sean's sleeping?"

"The couch?"

"Yep."

We bust out laughing.

"He's hoping they'll move out before school starts," Tyrell says. "But I don't think that's going to happen."

"Why not?"

"Because it's only three weeks away. We start before

Labor Day this year. At least the Minneapolis schools do. What about Saint Al's?"

"I'm not going back there."

"WHY? Don't be a fool."

"Can't. I got kicked out."

"No way. What happened?"

"I messed up."

"Too bad, Liam."

"No big deal. Seriously. I never belonged there anyway."

"Still. Where're you going to school?"

"Not sure right now." Should I tell him about art school? Can't yet. Might jinx everything.

"You don't want to go to Central, Liam. I know it's the clos-est to the JFKs, but that school's rough. Sean said a guy got stabbed in the eye with a plastic fork last year."

"I remember."

"Maybe you could get in at my charter school," Tyrell says.

"Yeah, you still like it there?"

"It's good, and it's in the hood. We'd probably be in the same college-prep program."

"Yeah. Cool."

"No school baseball team, though."

"After Saint Al's I don't even want to play for a high school anymore."

"We've still got our park team."

"Yep."

"Your mom should talk to my mom. Get all the info."

"I'll tell her," I say.

"Hey, what's up with your brother?"

"Which one?"

"Patrick."

"What do you mean?"

"Is he banging?" Tyrell says.

"What? Why?"

"I saw him down at the corner market. Irish Mafia took over that area. He was standing with that clown, Tommy."

"He told me he wasn't with those guys." I feel like I'm going to vomit. "You sure it was Patrick?"

"Yeah. Wearing a Boston Celtics shirt. Looked like he was a drug runner for the corner boys."

"What the —?"

"Every time a car would drive up for a buy, Patrick would go get the stuff," Tyrell says.

"Crap."

"Tried to talk to him, Liam. He told me to step off."

"I already got into it with him. We already discussed this mess."

"Patrick was with Tommy. I'm sure of it."

"SHITE! I told him to stay away from Irish Mafia."

"He's listening, man," Tyrell says. "Just not to you."

WRESTLING WITH WHAT TO DO

How do I keep Patrick out of danger?

Start sprinting up and down the beach.

Why, God? This isn't fair. Please. I got accepted. Found a place where I belong. Why are you letting all this other crap happen? I'm trying to be a better person. Now this stuff with Patrick. He lied to me. How am I supposed to know what to do? Shouldn't have to worry about all of this. Please make this go away. Please. Patrick isn't my responsibility. He's just my younger brother.

I stop running.

Tug on my holy medal. Rip it off my neck. Throw it as far away as I can. Out into Lake Michigan.

"GO TO HELL!" I throw a handful of wet sand up into the sky.

I was taught that you're always with us, God. That you never leave us. "WHERE ARE YOU NOW, HUH?" Because you don't seem to be with Patrick. And I thought you were by my side, but how can you be if you're not watching over my little brother?

I hate my life. Hate you too right now, God.

ACHING ALL OVER

From my episode at the beach yesterday. Body feels like I just played a doubleheader. Lost both games. Everything hurts. Especially my heart.

Look around my summer bedroom.

Not the one I share with Patrick and Declan.

Not the one that opens onto a parking lot.

Not the one on the eleventh floor of a project in a big city.

Not the one that Kieran used to share with us.

How long until Declan's got that room all to himself?

I get out of bed. Walk over to the window. Fog rolling in. Huge dark cloud. Appropriate. Spreading over the big lake. Covering everything. Just like a dirty sponge.

Crap of a day.

Get back in bed. The low moan of the foghorn begins. From the lighthouse. Beam of light shines around my room. No way.

"Are you kidding me?"

Struggling.

Believing.

Fighting.

Realizing.

Resisting.

Leaning.

Agonizing.

Accepting.

Rebelling.

Conforming.

Hating.

Loving.

Knowing what I'm going to do.

TELLING SARA

We sit outside the ice-cream place.

"I got accepted to Lake Michigan Academy of Fine Arts."
Still can't believe it.

She screams. "That's great." Hugs me.

"Not really."

"Why?"

"I can't stay."

"Why not?"

"I have to go back to Minneapolis."

"Liam."

"Patrick needs me."

"Your mom. Can't she take care of Pat—"

"No. It's not the same," I say. "And I'm not going to tell
her that I got accepted."

"Why?"

"I don't want her to know right now. She has no idea of
what's going on with Patrick."

"But I don't understand."

"You can't. You don't have any brothers or sisters. You
don't have to deal with the things we do because of where
we live."

"This is *your* opportunity to get away from there, Liam."

"I know there'll be more opportunities for me."

"Art school is such a great chance."

"I'm Patrick's older brother. He matters more than a chance."

RIDING THE WAVES

No use fighting. Let the water take me. Wherever it wants me to go. Like Saint Brendan. He questioned. Was angry with God, too. Went back onto the wild waves. Even though he was scared. He believed he would figure things out. He knew he'd find his way in the storms.

Saint Brendan the Navigator.

LETTING MOM KNOW

"I got my letter from Lake Michigan Academy of Fine Arts."

"Well? Drumroll . . ."

"I'm not going."

"*What?*"

"I didn't get accepted." Don't want her to worry about Patrick.

Silence.

"Mom?"

"Oh, Liam. I can't believe you didn't get in."

"No big deal." Yes, it is.

"I'm so sorry, honey."

"I know."

"Okay. So . . . umm. Okay," she says. "Well, school starts soon."

"Right." My summer's almost over.

"And Tyrell's mom told me about his charter school."

"Yeah."

"And there are some other good schools around—"

"I don't want to talk about schools right now, Mom."

"I know, honey. But we'll need to get something—"

"Please, Mom. Just tell Patrick I'll be back in Minneapolis next week."

"Okay." She sighs. "Well, at least you'll be back in time for your birthday."

"Yeah."

"It'll be nice to have you home."

Home?

"I love you, Liam."

"Love you, too."

RETURNING LIBRARY BOOKS

"Well, now I know why you were interested in the art books." Librarian smiles. "Your mural is absolutely beautiful, Liam."

"Glad you like it."

"Picasso and Basquiat would both be proud." She puts her hand out toward me. "Congratulations."

Shake her hand. "Thank you."

She picks up *The Chocolate War*. "So, what's your opinion?"

"I liked it."

She nods. "Because . . ."

"Mostly because Jerry did what he thought was right. Even when he knew it could turn out to be awful."

PEDALING TO THE ACADEMY

Kat's Coastie friend let me use his old-school beach bike. I want to take one last look around.

Ride to the top of the hill. Stop. Whole campus in front of me. Sand dunes on both sides. Big lake in front. Old and new buildings situated together. Look left. Behind the outdoor auditorium. There's the Visual Arts Center. Have to get there.

Fly down the hill. Wind tries to slow me. No. Faster. Pedal faster. Stomp back on the pedals. Slam the brakes. Tire skids across the sidewalk, makes a black line six feet long. Marking my territory.

Main doors are unlocked. Luck of the Irish. Enormous windows let the outside in and the inside out. Pay attention to every detail, O'Malley. Remember. I walk down the long hall. Ceramics. Sculpture. Drawing. Metals. Digital Arts. Photography. Printmaking. Fibers.

Last studio on the right. "Painting." Here it is. Chill climbs up my back. Can't go in. Can't not go in. Don't have a choice. This painting studio was mine. I was here. Belonged. I should be coming back. One of these stations was reserved for me. Can't come back. Remember everything about this place. Look. Smell. Touch. Every detail. Don't forget anything.

Lake Michigan Academy of Fine Arts was my chance. I took a chance, and they were willing to take a chance. Now it's ending. Am I making the wrong choice? Doesn't matter. Have to leave. Now.

Pedal back up the hill. Stop at the top. One last glance? No.

Don't look back.

HOLDING SARA'S HAND

"I'll miss you." Hate this.

She's crying. "Will you be back next summer?" Smiles through her tears.

"I'm not sure." My heart's going to drop out of my body.

"Liam . . ."

"I know." I hug her because I mean it.

STOPPING BY THE ROSE-COVERED HOUSE

"I'm leaving tomorrow, Hank."

"That's what I heard." He pats my back.

I nod.

"Yessir. Sure will be strange not seeing you around this small town."

"Yeah."

"You want some lemonade, Liam?"

"Sure." Not in any hurry.

We sit on his porch. Silence. Watch the boats anchored in the harbor.

"That'd be great to live out there." I point to my favorite sailboat. "Looks peaceful."

He rocks in his chair. "Liam, I want you to remember that a ship is safe in harbor—but that's not what ships are built for."

"I'm not sure what you mean."

"You will," Hank says. "You've got a good compass, young man."

WALKING A DIFFERENT SECTION OF THE BEACH

With Kat. Waiting for the sun to set. Waves pick up. Wash over my footprints. Makes it seem like I never walked in Lakeshore.

"Who's going to help you move the rest of your new sculpture?" I ask.

"Hmmm . . . I think I'll ask my carpenter friend. Remember you met him at dinner?"

"He's cool."

Wind picks up. Little kid plays tag with the waves. Back and forth.

"Wish I could see it when it's finished."

"Me too." She smiles. "I'll send you some photos."

"Okay."

The sun's sinking lower. We sit on the sand. Watch the huge ball of fire disappear into Lake Michigan. Just like my first night in Lakeshore.

"Kat . . . I . . ."

She puts her arm around my shoulder. "You have a home here, Liam. If you ever need anything. Or if you change your mind about arts school."

She knows? I haven't told her anything about Patrick.

"The admissions office inadvertently told me that you had phoned them to decline the acceptance. Something about a family situation?"

"Yeah. Patrick's been hanging out with Kieran's gang. I need to get home to try to help him. I don't know what I'm going to do, but I can't do anything from here."

"I have siblings, Liam. I understand."

"Did you tell my mom that I declined?"

"No. I figured you would let her know when the time is right. I trust your decision."

"Thank you." Relieved.

She turns toward me. "I admire your selflessness. You're a good older brother."

I nod.

"Keep me posted, okay?"

"Okay." Can't do this. Too much happening. Help.

"I love you, Liam. And I'm always here for you." She holds me close. "Never, ever forget that."

I cry.

PRAYING SLOWLY

I think of Saint Brendan's dying words:

> *I fear that I shall journey alone, that the way will be dark;*
> *I fear the unknown land, the presence of my King and the*
> *sentence of my judge.*

I fear my journey, too. Don't know what's going to happen in Minneapolis.

Think about all the pieces of Saint Brendan's life.

He was scared. He went anyway. Didn't have any choice.

> *Shall I take my tiny boat across the wide sparkling ocean? O*
> *King of the Glorious Heaven, shall I go of my own choice*
> *upon the sea? O Christ, will You help me on the wild waves?*

Please be with Patrick until I get home, God.

Tug on my . . . Crap. Medal's gone. I pitched it into Lake Michigan.

Please be with me, too.

"Saint Brendan, pray for me."

IMAGINING EMPTY WALLS AT HOME

Think of Minneapolis. Not the worst place in the world. Have to keep looking forward. Focus on my art. Check out that graffiti-mentoring opportunity. Try to convince someone to let me paint a mural somewhere at home, too. Something that reflects my aesthetic. Maybe something influenced by the work of Diego Rivera. Use spray paint if I want.

Get inspiration from my hood. Create my own thing. Not cubism. Not something that hangs on a wall in a museum. Just ordinary, everyday life. Things that happen all the time in the projects. Good and bad. Beautiful and ugly.

Social Realism.

Created by someone who knows what's real.

A street artist who's tired of being tagged by everyone who doesn't know him.

Hoping for a fresh canvas.

HOLDING PATTERN OVER MINNEAPOLIS

Plane's circling around downtown. Can't land just yet. Close my blackbook. Nothing but skyscrapers down there. Same buildings Tyrell, Sean, and I see from the roof of the JFKs. Target Field right below the plane. Twins are playing. Afternoon game against the Red Sox.

"Ladies and gentlemen, we are now flying over Minneapolis. The captain has turned the seatbelt signs back on. We are in our final descent and will be landing shortly."

Gliding over the chain of city lakes. They look more like ponds to me now. People everywhere. Skateboarding. Rollerblading. Swimming. Walking. Running. Biking. Some trees. Some sand.

No lighthouses.

Coming back to my hood. Lots more concrete. Parks. Projects. People. All thrown together in a heap.

Big city. Big projects. Small lakes.

Different from Lakeshore, but it's the place I know by heart.

FOLLOWING MY COMPASS

I'm back where I belong.

Walking through the airport. Surrounded by a huge crowd. Energy vibrating through my feet. Feels good. Down the escalator to luggage claim. What now?

"LIAM!" The O'Malley family greets me. Declan's jumping up and down. Fiona's making weird faces. Mom's waving. Patrick stands behind the group.

He looks okay. Not wearing any Irish Mafia crap.

Hugs from Mom and the little kids.

Homie hug for Patrick. He seems taller. But still has to look up to me. "How's it going?"

"Okay." He cracks his knuckle. "Welcome home."

"Thanks." Grab my Crusaders baseball duffel bag.

"Liam! Liam! Here's my brachiosaurus." Declan shoves it in my face.

"Very cool."

"Hey!" Fiona jabs her finger into my chest. She reads the logo on my shirt. "What's Lake Michigan Academy of Fine Arts?"

"A place I went this summer. An arts camp."

"Are you an artist or something?" She stares.

I smile. Am I an artist? "Yes."

"That's a lot better than being a *prisoner*, sheesh!"

Same ol' shit.

"Oh, before I forget." Mom pulls a brochure out of her purse. "Take a look at this."

There are awesome designs on the cover. Great colors. "Minneapolis Fine Arts High School?" I look at Mom. "In Minneapolis?"

"Downtown. And registration is still open for this year."

Nod. Don't know what to say. "Ummm . . ."

"We can schedule a meeting and a tour if you think you're interested."

"Okay, but . . ."

"Mom!" Fiona interrupts. "Declan made his dinosaur bite me."

"No, I didn't!"

"We can talk about it later." Mom pats my back. "I've got to get you four home, and then I have to be at Kieran's pre-trial hearing by three thirty."

I follow my family out the doors. Fiona and Declan argue about who saw me first. Mom searches for the keys to the minivan. Patrick's three steps in front of me. My kid brother. I match his stride. Step for step. I have his back. It feels good to be home.

I think.

I hope.

From Lakeshore to Minneapolis in the blink of an eye. Was it a dream? Back to my hood. JFKs. Back to not knowing what's around the corner. Back to being with my family. My friends.

This is my real life. What next?

Empty walls are waiting to see what I have to say.

ACKNOWLEDGMENTS

Monumental thanks to my editor, Julie Bliven, for passing me the ball again and again until I finally made the winning shot. You, and your assists, are the best. I dig you like an old soul record!

Colossal thanks to my agent, Joan Paquette, for believing in all my work and for finding the perfect home for Liam's story. I'm so happy you're in my corner. You're a gem!

Heartfelt gratitude for the part each of you have played in making my dream come true: Megan C. Atwood, Marsha Wilson Chall, Francine Conley, Sue Ellen Cooper, Karen Bonnici Czarnik, Cecilia Konchar Farr, Antonia Felix, Pamela Fletcher, Paula Foreman, Kristin Gallagher, Molly Beth Griffin, Hamline University's MFA in Writing for Children and Young Adults and MA in Liberal Studies programs, Gay Herzberg, Carol Hodgkin, Kristin Hoefling, Ron Koertge, Debbie Kovacs, Laurel Learmonth, Mary Logue, Magers & Quinn Booksellers, Waive McDonald, Minneapolis street artists, Claire Rudolf Murphy, Don Nelson, Lon Otto, Joy Lehto Paeth, Penelope Phelps, Laurie Pickett, Marie Prsynski, Marsha Qualey, Nicole Rasmussen, Mary Rockcastle, Saint Catherine University, Anita Silvey, Sojourner Project (Holly and Rachel), Caren Stelson, Lennon Sundance, Betsy Thomas, Pamela

Trier, Anne Ursu, Jody Van Riper, Western Michigan University, Walker Art Center (especially my fellow gallery guards), Tina Wexler, Leslie Keeley White, and Wild Rumpus Books for Young Readers.

And last, but definitely not least, to my family: Kyle, Maggie, Mom, Dad, Jill, Bob, Joe, Julie, and Brody. Thank you for your unconditional love and support and for continually encouraging me to follow my own path. Words cannot express . . .

READER'S GROUP GUIDE

1. Why is the title of the novel significant? Does the meaning change throughout the story?

2. There are several instances throughout where Liam expresses his desire to prove he exists. Why is this important to Liam? What does this say about his situation?

3. Why does Liam agree to help Kieran? What are his feelings about his brother?

4. On page 24, why does the owner of the corner market yell at Liam and his siblings on their way to school?

5. Why does the other JFK boy at Saint Al's tell Liam he's throwing away his chance? Why does he care?

6. Take a look at page 32. Talk about the formatting of the text. How does it reflect the character's emotional state? What is the significance of this scene following Liam's meeting with the headmaster?

7. On page 36, Liam describes his mother's eyes as being huge. What do you think that means? What can be assumed about his mother's actions?

8. What is the significance of a tag? Why would Los Crooks be willing to kill Liam because of the tag he did for Kieran? Would they be willing to kill him because of his St. B tag?

9. Why do you think Liam connects so strongly with Saint Brendan the Navigator?

10. What is happening when Liam says one thing in his dialog but thinks another in the narrative? What does that tell you about Liam's character?

11. On page 42, Liam is hanging out on the roof when shots ring out in the street below. Sean and Tyrell treat it like a game. What does this tell you about their lives? Does Liam still think it's a game?

12. Liam has trust issues. What are some instances in the story that reveal this? Whom does Liam trust?

13. How do you interpret Liam's response to the Claes Oldenburg quote on page 63?

14. The chapter that begins on page 87 is titled "Deciding to Waste My Life Again." What does Liam mean by this? What do you suppose are his reasons for tagging *St. B* in Lakeshore?

15. Why does Liam open up to Kat about what happened to him on the baseball team?

16. Consider both sides of Sara and Liam's argument about graffiti. Who's right? Do you think that graffiti is an art form or a crime? Why?

17. Liam worries about becoming an artist and losing what it means to be a graffiti writer. How would he define both pursuits? What is the difference that bothers him?

18. On page 215, what does Liam mean when he thinks, "Need to keep him out of the wreck"?

19. How is Liam's removal of the *St. B* tags symbolic?

20. What role does friendship play in *Tagged*? What about family?